CRESCENT PROPHECY

THE CRESCENT WITCH CHRONICLES -
BOOK TWO

NICOLE R. TAYLOR

CHAPTER 1

Sitting behind the counter of Irish Moon, the crystal shop I owned and ran in the small Irish village of Derrydun, I lazily shuffled my tarot cards.

Summer was coming to an end, and with it, marked my first three months as a new resident of Ireland.

When my mother had passed—the same mother who abandoned my late father and me when I was two years old—I was drawn to Ireland to claim my inheritance. The cottage and Irish Moon I knew about, but a more mysterious legacy had revealed itself in the most unexpected way.

Thinking about all the things that had happened since I first arrived in the little Irish village, I smiled. It hadn't exactly been smooth sailing.

It had all started when Robert O'Keeffe, the lawyer of my mother, Aileen, turned up and zapped me with his golden pen. It wasn't as dirty as it sounded because that zap had unbound my magic.

Yep, I was a Crescent Witch. The last in a long line of badasses who protected the magical creatures of Ireland,

and now it was my turn to protect Derrydun and its hawthorn trees.

Outside the window, I caught a glimpse of a handsome Irishman wearing a black and red checkered shirt. Boone. He was cutting back Mrs. Boyle's—the unpredictable old lady who loved whacking people with her broom—hedges.

Boone... Well, he was another story. He turned out to be a shapeshifter with amnesia.

Seeing your crush turn into a fox, then a gyrfalcon, and a tabby cat, kind of made things impossible to deny.

Add that in with my life in Australia falling apart—my boyfriend Alex dumping me and being handed a redundancy package from my employer. Then throw in a pinch of my witch legacy, a battle with a grotesque monster, almost being drowned by a bunch of shadow people, and my estranged mother being killed by a trickster fae called a spriggan and not a run-of-the-mill heart attack, and there you had the last four months of my life. One big ball of W.T.F.

Oh, yeah, and the whole magic double life? Only Boone and I knew. To everyone else, I was just a weirdo in a crystal shop, and Boone was the sweetheart of Derrydun. He didn't know where he'd come from before landing in the village, and no one cared. He could do no wrong, which had been infuriating for an outsider like me, but I'd since been accepted into the fold. Derrydun had claimed me, magically and 'Irishly.'

The tarot cards were heavy in my hands, and I placed the deck on the countertop. They were a pretty set of black cards with metallic gold artwork and had been a favorite of my mother. They were one of the few things I knew about Aileen and something I had found comfort in during the tumble dryer my life had become.

The cards were not meant to see the future but act as words of wisdom and guidance for the journey ahead. Something that had come in handy a lot lately.

The Tower had brought me here, and The Star had given me hope that things had been rebuilt enough, and now I could now look forward to a future of discovery and stability. At least for the time being.

Glancing at the clock on the wall, I frowned. Mairead was late today. She was the seventeen-year-old shop assistant who helped me here at Irish Moon. Since it was her last day before she went off to Trinity College in Dublin, I would give her a pass.

She was a moody Goth girl, who had an epic crush on my newly acquired boyfriend, Boone. I'd forgiven her weeks ago for tricking him into giving her a kiss as payment for looking after the shop when I was sick. *Sick* being the covert word for totally depleting my magical reserves healing Boone when he ran afoul of a craglorn. The awful creature that wouldn't have even been stalking the village had it not been for my carelessness.

Long story short, I owed him one—hence the healing —and in repayment, he'd planted his lips on Mairead. You better believe I'd made him suffer.

Speaking of… The door thrust open, the bell jangling furiously, and Mairead stormed through the shop and disappeared out back to dump her bag. She looked nice today, her usual Goth attire ramped up to ten. Black boots, shiny black leggings, black top with white skulls printed on it, and a long black cardigan. When she reemerged, I smiled.

"Last day. Glad to get rid of me?" I asked, scooping up the tarot cards.

She rolled her eyes and pouted, her black lipstick

making her skin look paler than the ivory of her makeup already did. Hugging a black folder against her chest, she sighed dramatically.

I'd learned not to take her moody Goth attitude to heart because hers was always in the right place. How many times had she chastised me since arriving? Too many to count. Ultimately, it was the Crescent Witch legacy that forced me to stay, but it had been one of Mairead's teenage tantrums that had sealed the deal and made me see that it wasn't all that bad here.

"I drew a card for you this morning," I went on, waving the tarot deck. "It was the bitch card."

"*Very funny.*"

"What's that you've got there?"

"I made this for you," she said, handing me the display book.

Flipping open the cover, I leafed through the silky plastic pockets, my eyebrows raising. It was an Irish Moon employee handbook. Mairead had actually sat down at a computer, typed out the shop procedures, printed it out, and put all the pages in the pockets. There was even a contents page.

"You did all this?" My mouth fell open, and I glanced at her.

"Can't have Aileen's shop fallin' into chaos the moment I leave," she said with a shrug. Her cheeks were turning redder by the minute. She pretended to be aloof, but she lapped up the praise, secretly loving the achievement. We'd become a mismatched pair of buddies somewhere along the track, her and me.

"You think I can't handle this place on my own? I can get Boone to help. He's already got a thousand different jobs, so one more won't hurt him."

"Do you really want to spend all your time with him?" she asked. "You don't want to get tired of each other. Others are linin' up."

"What, now you're finally about to turn eighteen, you're a relationship expert?" I asked with a snort.

"I'd hate for you to give up lips like those." She smiled sweetly.

I gasped dramatically. "Oh, no, you didn't!"

"You may have caught him, but at least I still got a kiss."

I rolled my eyes and tossed her the feather duster.

Boone was ten years her senior, or at least, we thought he was, and she'd had a crush on him ever since he turned up in Derrydun. Me arriving had only thrown a spanner in the works of her grand plan to bag an older man.

"You're about to go to college in Dublin," I said. "You'll forget about Boone the moment you find a hot guy who's into spider webs."

"I'm going to miss your jokes," she shot back. "*Not.*"

"Now, there's some important information I must impart to you before you leave. It's been passed down from woman to woman, over generations dating back to the land before time. A very important thing to remember when you're out in the world on your own for the first time."

"Oh, yeah? And what's that?"

"*Don't forget to use protection.*"

"Skye!" the girl exclaimed, rolling her eyes.

"Don't say I didn't warn you when you get an itchy—"

The door opened, and the bell jingled as Boone walked in, looking just as irritated as Mairead did.

"It must be feather-up-the-butt day," I declared. "What's tickling you?"

"Ack, I'm givin' myself a headache," he exclaimed, scratching his head.

His wild, curly, almost black hair fell into his eyes, the haircut I'd given him the week before already grown out. He looked hot with his short back and sides and mop on top.

"Overthinking again?" I asked, eyeing Mairead.

We'd had this discussion before, Boone and I. A side effect of his memory loss was giving himself a migraine every time he tried to remember something about his forgotten past. Which meant his amnesia was magically induced. He'd told me Aileen had tried to remove the block but hadn't been able to move it at all. Apparently, the verdict was, only the person who put it there in the first place could remove it. And that was totally useful information. *Not.*

"Nay, Sean is givin' me a ribbin' again."

Sean McKinnon was the closest thing Boone had to a best mate. They worked together for Roy at his farm just outside of the village and spent a great deal of money over at the local pub, Molly McCreedy's. Sean's wife had died from cancer a few years ago, and he'd become the town drunk as a result. He'd never really gotten over her passing, and Boone seemed to be the only person able to keep him from completely drowning in sorrow.

"The busybody," I grumbled.

"And Mary says spring is a great month, but summer could also work."

My mouth fell open. The village hadn't let up with the gossiping ever since they'd seen Boone and I give each other a little kiss out front of Irish Moon. You would think a few weeks would give them time to cool down about it, but no. Looked like they were already planning the wedding.

Mairead snorted, and I glared at her in warning. Turning, she began to dust the shelves while pretending not to listen in.

"It's only been a month," I said. "I don't know about you, but I haven't had a chance to catch my breath yet."

"I know."

"I don't know what you want me to do about it," I said. "They'll tire of it eventually."

"Eventually isn't soon enough."

"You're the one who never went out with anyone, so now that you have, of course, it's going to be the talk of the village. The coveted has finally been claimed. It's a small place. There isn't much else to do but make a melodrama out of everything."

"You don't seem worried about it," he complained. "Especially with the…" He glanced at Mairead. "*The thing.*"

"Aileen managed it," I whispered, referring to her duty to the Crescents. "So can we. Just let them have their fun, and things will die down."

"How is that goin', by the way?"

"Just as shambolic as always."

"Have you been goin' to the hawthorn?"

"Of course, I have."

"Good."

"This is so weird," I declared, raising my voice to give Mairead something to listen to. "This should be the other way around. Me complaining and you telling me to build a bridge."

"Aye, I know, I know." He leaned against the counter

and nudged the tarot cards. "Have you drawn anythin' good today?"

"The Page of Pentacles," I replied. "This dude likes to learn new shite, so I guess he's fitting, huh?"

"It's a good sign." He glanced at Mairead, then back to me. "I've got to get to work."

"Mary's Teahouse today?"

"The one and the same." He leaned over the counter and gave me an awkward kiss on the cheek. "I'll see you tonight."

I watched him leave the shop and wander across the street to the bright pink cottage with the thatched roof. We were close, there was no denying it, but when it came to public displays of affection, Boone sucked. It was like going out with a teenage boy with zero experience who was stuck in the body of a full-grown man. *A man who could change into a tabby cat.*

"So awkward," Mairead said, standing by the window.

"Shut up." I made a face.

"Seriously, I think I dodged a bullet."

Yeah, right.

"Hey, before I forget…" I reached under the counter and found the box I'd put there that morning. "Here. Something to remember us by." Offering her the box, she glanced at me warily, and I shook it. "Hurry up before I change my mind."

Crossing the shop floor, she took the little red box from my fingers and cracked open the lid. I watched her with a smile as she saw the little golden quartz crystal pendant inside.

"It's just like yours," she said.

"Sure. They're best friend charms."

It was really a talisman I'd spelled for protection, hence

the golden flecks in the once clear piece of quartz. This time, I'd gone to the hawthorn in the forest to cast the spell rather than sit out in the open. My little crystal was the beginning of all our problems with the craglorn. By casting the spell outside the protection of the hawthorn, I'd sent up a flare, which attracted any wayward fae in the area, that I was a juicy buffet of magic just waiting to be sucked dry. Starving fae and tender, ripe witch equaled disaster. There was no way I was making that mistake again.

Anyway, it was a much smoother cast this time. I was more experienced and only used a little of my witch juju. I totally felt like a spring lamb afterward rather than having to take a nap among the rhododendron at the tower house.

"They so aren't," Mairead complained.

"No, not really. It's a talisman," I said, smiling. "It's a special quartz crystal for protection."

"Cool." She tried to sound nonchalant about it, but immediately put the chain over her head.

"We'll miss you, Mairead," I said. "You're welcome to come back anytime."

"Yeah, right. You'll replace me the second I'm gone."

"You keep telling yourself that," I quipped.

CHAPTER 2

I rish Moon was deathly quiet.

Sitting behind the counter, my shoulders sagged as I surveyed the empty shop. Crystals glittered under the lights, the rack of wind chimes was still, the bookcase was dusted and rearranged, the tumbled stones were tumbled, the jewelry cabinet was dusted and reorganized, and still, I was bored out of my mind.

I'd gotten used to having Mairead around in the shop. After a summer with her pouty Goth face and smartass one-liners, I was starting to become lonely with just myself for company. Not even Boone's daily visit chased away all of the doldrums. I was also starting to realize how much she actually did around the place. Her employee handbook was coming in real handy.

So, after a week without any help, and almost driving both Boone and myself mad, I finally scheduled some job interviews.

Sitting among the crystals in Irish Moon, I felt their energy shining on me like a heat lamp. Glancing at the stack of resumes in my lap, I knew I was going to need every good vibe that came my way. I'd drawn the Knight of Cups that morning, but so far, my knight in shining armor hadn't appeared.

After seeing a woman who was clearly drunk, a guy who clearly had a flair for woman's clothing, a farmer's wife who tracked mud through the shop, and a girl who needed a job for brownie points with her parole officer, I was beginning to lose hope. The whole day was like a hilarious montage from a movie until finally, the perfect person showed up.

Lucy Sutton had one hell of a resume, and I was more interested in finding out why she wanted a job as my sidekick. Granted, she didn't know about the witch stuff, so on paper, I was just the owner of a New Age shop in the middle of nowhere. No one in their right mind would willingly ditch a big city to come here…unless they wanted to get away from something.

When she arrived, I was expecting her to be dressed in a mixture of camo gear with a safari hat and a rifle slung over her shoulder for shooting lions, but she was the epitome of boho sheik.

Her long strawberry-blonde hair was loose and wavy, her green eyes were made all the more brilliant by the mass of freckles over her entire face—she gave Maggie over at Molly McCreedy's a run for her money—and her outfit was a layered tie-dye dress over blue jeans and boots. She totally had a seventies flower child vibe but didn't look a day over thirty.

"Hi, are you Skye?" she asked with a thick Irish accent.

"The one and the same. You must be Lucy?"

"Aye, that's me. I hope I'm not too early."

"We like early around here," I said, smiling. "Have a seat."

She slid onto the chair beside mine, her gaze darting around Irish Moon with unmasked curiosity.

"Tell me about yourself," I began.

"Well… I studied archaeology, anthropology, and folklore at Trinity College in Dublin," she said. "Since graduatin', I've worked on a few exhibitions around the country and a couple of excavations, but nothing long-term. I've been workin' at Debenhams in Galway."

"You're Indiana Jones, and you've been working in a department store?" I asked, making a face.

She laughed and shook her head. "It's not like that, though, it would be a thrill. Paid work is hard to come by, and when somethin' does come up, it's rather competitive. There's only so much volunteerin' I can do before the rent is due."

"Galway is a fair way to come for a job," I mused.

"Oh, I know. I don't mind movin'. Been doin' it me whole life."

I peered at her resume again and frowned. There was no logical reason why she would want to take a job selling New Age knickknacks to tourists when she could do a hundred other things. Like work in a museum or dig up ancient burial sites like *Lara Croft: Tomb Raider*. Seriously, why wasn't she in the Amazon looking for El Dorado?

"Why do you want to work at a crystal shop in the ass end of nowhere?" I asked, voicing my thoughts. "Surely, there are more exciting places you can go?"

"I suppose so, but I don't want to leave Ireland." She shrugged. "Out here is where the history lives, you know? There's a ruined tower house on your doorstep, so it doesn't get any closer than that. I can earn money doin' somethin' I'm interested in and be among history."

This woman was too good to be true. She was like the

ready-made librarian, know-it-all sidekick out of *Buffy The Vampire Slayer*. The guy who knew everything because of books. What's-his-name. The plot device needed to fill all the holes with his superior book smarts. Just what this story needed!

"It gets busy in here," I said, giving her the rundown of what I needed. "Derrydun is a stop on most of the bus tours, so don't let the calm before the storm fool you. I have commitments that sometimes drag me away unexpectedly, so there'll be times I might have to leave you to manage the place alone. You good with that?"

She shrugged. "Sure. Galway is the same with the tour buses, and I don't mind working alone. I like to be busy."

"And we're strange around here."

"Aren't all the best people?"

I threw my hands up in the air. "You say all the right things. When can you start?"

"Tomorrow?"

"It's a date!" I declared. "See you at ten a.m. sharp."

After seeing Lucy out, I watched her cross the street, pass under the hawthorn growing in the middle of the road, and get into a little blue car parked by Mary's Teahouse. The tree didn't move, and I frowned.

When I'd first arrived in Derrydun, Boone told me the hawthorn had bent toward me, its leaves attracted to my magic like a magnet. I'd almost expected it to reveal something about Lucy as she passed beneath its branches, but not even a breeze stirred its limbs.

I wasn't sure what I was expecting, but it wasn't that. It had been too easy, her walking in here with her stellar resume and boho hippy sheik. She was perfect for the job, and I needed someone to run things when a witchy crisis was in full swing, so why was I all wound up about it?

Maybe all this Crescent Witch destiny stuff was making me paranoid.

I shook my head as a big white tour bus came around the bend and began to slowly navigate its way around the hawthorn.

Maybe there was a way to make sure she wasn't a wolf in sheep's clothing or so to speak. I'd been attacked by a wolf—which were meant to be extinct in Ireland—almost gutted by a twisted fae with giant claws, escaped a near drowning by a bunch of Sluagh—shadow fae who ate peoples' souls for a living—and almost put myself into a magical coma when I used all of my magic to heal Boone. I was definitely not going to be brought down by an unemployed archaeologist.

I had to be sure. Right? The last Crescent Witch couldn't take any chances, not when the existence of magic hung in the balance.

When I got back to the cottage that night, I retrieved the spell book from underneath the floorboards in the bedroom and brought it downstairs. Sitting on the couch—with its awful floral and beige color scheme—I began studying the pages.

Lucy was way too good to be true. I had an uneasy feeling, but I wasn't sure if it was my gut talking or the lingering doom and gloom of the battle for magic giving me a complex. There had to be a way to know for sure if she was a fae or under the influence of one.

The spells at the beginning of the book were written in Irish and Latin, the pages were wobbly and brown with age, and the further I went, the clearer the words became.

It was a trip through time, though how long ago was anyone's guess.

I hoped I would be smart enough to put a spell of my own in there one day. After experiencing the magic I unleashed when I was fighting the craglorn, I knew it was in me. It was just putting it on paper that was the problem. I didn't know which words to use to describe the instinct I'd used, let alone what kind of spell would be useful. You couldn't teach love. It just was.

The front door opened and banged shut, revealing Boone. He stomped his feet on the mat and kicked off his boots before shuffling into the lounge room.

"Ah, here comes the Iron Chef," I said, hinting I wanted him to cook dinner. It was the only way he was going to get a meal that wasn't microwaved.

"What's an iron chef?" he asked, sitting beside me.

"It's this show that used to be on one of the TV channels back home," I explained. "From an Asian country, I can't remember which. It was a game show where chefs competed against one another in an arena."

"What did they win?"

"They won the title of *Iron Chef. Duh.*"

"That's it?"

"What do you mean, 'that's it?'" I air quoted the last part.

"Surely, they won cash and prizes. I thought that was the point of those programs."

"Surely, the achievement is worth more than money and a bunch of stuff," I said with a pout. "Don't mess with *Iron Chef.* It has a cult following, you know."

"You're weird."

"I'm weird? You're the fox in human's clothing."

Boone puffed out his chest and winked. "Aye, I am a bit of a fox if I do say so myself."

"Can you change into a pig?" I made a face.

"Very funny."

Turning back to the spell book, I began flicking through the pages again. Tracing my fingers over worn handwriting and diagrams, I tried to piece together a plan.

"What are you doin'?" Boone asked, looking at me like I'd sprouted a second head.

"I want to see if there's a way I can test her," I muttered.

"Test who for what?"

"Lucy."

"Who's Lucy?"

"The woman I hired to help at Irish Moon. I want to see if I can test her to make sure she's not a fae."

"Skye, I think you're makin' too much out of this. Hundreds of tourists come through the village every week, and none of them have been fae. Not everyone is out to get you. Besides, the hawthorns…"

"We can't be too careful," I argued. "Look at what happened with that Hannah chick. She turned out to be a spriggan, and Aileen didn't even know. The hawthorns didn't help then, and we can't rely on the trees all the time." Boone stiffened at my offhanded comment about the fae that had killed my mother. She was trying to save him at the time, and it had once been a sore point between us, but now there were bigger fish to fry. "After everything that happened with the craglorn and everything that will happen with Carman *eventually*, I can't take any chances."

"I don't think—"

"If she's a spy, then I want to know."

He grunted, and I set the spell book aside. Nestling closer, I laid my hand over his and squeezed.

"Boone, I'm the last Crescent. And if I believe everything you've told me and all the shite in this book, then I'm the only one who can kick Carman's ass. I'm pretty sure it was my ancestors who banished her from Ireland and locked the doors to the fae realm. I may not be the Crescent who did those things, but I'm the only one around for her to take revenge on. If I'm out of the picture, nothing will stand in her way. She'll crawl back in and unleash whatever power lingers on the other side." I sighed. And if she succeeded, magic would be extinct, and the world would be defenseless in the face of the fae realm. "It's so *dramatic*, but you know. Priorities."

What was on the other side of the doors, anyway? Why did the Crescents lock them for good? Knowing my luck, it was to protect Earth from being invaded by a mystical army of fairies. That was usually how those stories went. The desire for ultimate power and chaos weren't an exclusively human trait.

"Aye, well, just be careful. Don't go turnin' her into a toad."

My eyes widened. "I can turn people into toads?"

Boone frowned and cupped my face. Leaning forward, he kissed me. His touch was soft at first, but when tongue was added to the mix, the heat level rose. Just when things were borderline indecent, he pulled away.

"What would you like for dinner?" he asked, dumping a proverbial bucket of ice water on my head.

"A cock sandwich," I retorted, completely frustrated.

"A what?"

"A *cooked* sandwich," I said, scowling and picking up the

spell book. "Like a nice slab of satisfying meat slapped between some bread."

It was a metaphor that went right over Boone's clueless head, and he shrugged. Ever since I'd woken from my post-healing three-day sleep and we'd fallen into our romantic relationship, it had been awkward as hell. It was like he didn't even know how to be affectionate or act normal around me. In the wake of me discovering my magic and his shapeshifter-ness, our easy friendship had stalled. Something wasn't right, and I didn't know how to fix it.

It didn't help that I was still trying to understand the new world I was thrown into, manage a business with zero book smarts, *and* find a new employee. I was building a new life from scratch, and it hadn't been that long since I was dumped by my last boyfriend and lost my job in a supernatural conspiracy to get me back to the ancestral home of the Crescents.

I needed Boone. Honestly, I needed him in more ways than a pillar of strength in the chaos. I needed him *all night long*, but he didn't seem to get it. Considering it was the one thing men always knew everything about, it was way more annoying than the entire population of Derrydun planning our supposed spring wedding.

Boone disappeared into the kitchen, leaving me to wonder if I should be studying the spell book or going online to order myself a dildo.

And when he reappeared half an hour later, guess what he had made me for dinner?

A lamb sandwich.

CHAPTER 3

Fiddling absently with my tarot cards, I watched Lucy from behind the counter.

After a morning of showing her the ins and outs of Irish Moon, I was happy to see her busying herself with tidying the shop and familiarizing herself with the stock. At least she was showing more enthusiasm than I had when I first arrived, but I suppose she'd come here wanting the job in the first place. Unlike me.

She'd been early, too. It was like a vortex where everything was reversed. Lucy was the complete opposite of me, which was probably a good thing considering I liked to sleep in and laze about behind the counter.

"Do you read tarot cards?" she asked, watching me shuffle.

"I've been learning," I replied. "They were my mother's cards."

"Were?" Lucy crossed the shop floor and stood on the other side of the counter.

"She died a few months ago." I shrugged. "I inherited the shop and her house."

"Oh, I'm sorry. I didn't know." She shook out her hair to hide her reddening cheeks. "Way to go askin' the personal questions on me first day."

"It's fine. We weren't really close. Meaning, I never really knew her when she was here. She left my dad and me when I was little and…"

Realizing I was babbling to a suspected spy, I closed my mouth and shrugged. I was becoming really paranoid. Didn't help that Lucy was easy to talk to. She had one of those faces, which could be a trick or a spell or anything.

"So you and your dad lived in Australia?"

I nodded.

"How long have you been in Ireland for? Do you like it here?"

"I've been here about five months now, I think. A lot has happened. A lot of readjusting." That was the understatement of the century.

"So how does this tarot thing work?" she went on, thankfully changing the subject. "I've never had them done before."

"Well, people think they're for telling the future, but they're more for guidance and intuition than anything. They can help you think about the situation you're in and guide you toward making a decision. Life lessons." I raised my eyebrows.

They'd given me plenty of 'lessons' in the past few months. The Tower heralded the destruction of my world's order and the rebuilding of my life in Derrydun. The Star had followed, cropping up in multiple readings to remind me of renewed hope after I'd found out I was a witch. Since then, the cards had been random and confusing, and no reoccurring trends had cropped up. I suppose it meant I was in a period of normality. Which was a good thing for someone like me.

"Would you do me?" Lucy asked.

"What?" I pulled a face.

"A card, a card," she exclaimed, flapping her hands about. "I'm not propositionin' you! Oh, God, I did not just say that."

I laughed and shook my head. "That's nothing. You should've heard some of the things Mairead used to say."

"Who?"

"The girl who worked here before you." Placing the cards on the counter, I swept the deck along the surface, fanning out the black and gold rectangles. "Now think about what you would like the cards to reveal to you, then choose one from wherever."

Lucy thought for a moment, then reached out and slid a card from the spread. Turning it over, she said, "Oh, this looks cool."

Taking the card, I saw it was the Ace of Wands. Traditionally, this card had an image of a hand emerging from a cloud, grasping a wand that was still growing, its length covered in new shoots and flowers, signifying a blossoming development. In the background, there was usually a castle to represent the promise of what opportunities were possible in the future. In this deck, the image was different, but it still had the same representations. The wand was the center focus, its length also covered with leaves, but at the top was the flame of inspiration. In the foreground were flowers and rolling fields, lush with the promise of a prosperous future…if one was intuitive enough to reach out and take it.

"The Wands are a good suit," I explained. "They are all about creativity, strength, and inspiration. The Ace is to do with inspiration, power, beginnings, and potential. It's pretty much a sign that says, go for it."

"That's good." Lucy blew out a breath, and her shoulders sank, losing some of the tension she'd been holding.

"It's a really good card, to be honest. It's saying that you're inspired by a new project and to listen to your instincts. But…"

"Oh, there's always a but."

"That's where the life lesson comes in," I said with a chuckle. "The Ace is also reminding you that your inspiration is still only a seed. There's still a long way to go, but if you nurture it, it could grow into something very good. Which is great for me, by the way."

Lucy laughed, and her eyes sparkled. Whatever nervousness she'd been carrying seemed to have disappeared, and despite my fears she was a trickster fae in the service of Carman, I was really liking her. *Dammit.*

Our conversation petered out, and she turned back to the shop and made herself busy. Watching her, I shuffled the tarot cards and drew one for myself. Seeing the card, I groaned. *Great, just great.* Why couldn't I get the Ace of bloody Wands?

The Three of Swords stared back at me, and I glared at the image of three blades piercing a heart with a teary eye in the center. Heartbreak, betrayal, grief, rejection, separation. Not good. Something was coming, but I knew it was. It was just a matter of when and if it had anything to do with the arrival of my new shop assistant.

Lucy had made herself busy by emptying out each little container of tumbled stones and dusting them out before placing all the colored crystals back. First was the citrine— which was a curious choice as citrine was for wealth and prosperity—then the amethyst, rose quartz, snowflake obsidian, and fluorite.

Seeing she was completely engrossed, I saw a chance at nabbing the final ingredient for my patchwork fae identification spell. Rounding the counter, I pretended to tidy the knickknacks on the counter—cheap bracelets, New Agey postcards, and Irish-themed trinkets—and worked my way closer. I just had to reach out and pluck a hair from her wild mane of strawberry-blonde waves, and it would do the trick. I just had to plonk it in the potion, and it would change color just like a drug test but without the pee in the jar.

Just as I was inches from my target, I caught sight of Boone through the window. He pointed at Lucy and mouthed, "Is that her?" Giving him a pointed look, I made a cutting motion across my neck. He was going to blow my cover.

Lucy turned and caught me gesturing at Boone, and her mouth dropped open. "Who's that, and where can I get one?"

"*That* is my boyfriend," I retorted, annoyed he'd shown up and ruined my chance at snapping up a strand of her hair.

Boone made a face and hurried away, likely knowing he would face my wrath later on. He wasn't exactly on board with the whole fae test, which was mystifying as he was always the one to chastise me for fiddling with magic away from the hawthorns. I was desperate to have a house full of magically automated utensils to take over all the jobs I hated. Like drying the dishes, stirring pots on the stove, hanging out the washing, *folding* the washing, and so on. But I wasn't allowed since, you know, the war for magic and the lingering threat of craglorns coming to suck out witches' power and turning us into mummified husks and stuff. Which brought me back to my first argument—Boone was mad for dismissing my need to confirm Lucy's orientation. Fae, human, or otherwise influenced.

"So hot," Lucy said, fanning herself. "Lucky you! Does he have a brother?"

"No, luckily for me, there's only one of him." One with many furry faces.

"Shame," she said with a sigh. "I would've asked you to set me up."

"No boyfriend, huh?"

She shook her head.

Thinking about last night's lamb sandwich, I curled my lip. It wasn't happily ever after once people got together, that was for sure. After the kiss and the declaration of feelings and all that soppy shite was when the *real* work began.

We were so engrossed in boy talk that when the bell above the door rang, we both jumped a mile. Turning, all the blood drained from my face when I saw who it was.

He was shorter than Boone by a head, his skin bronzed from years playing Aussie Rules football out in the Australian sun. His hair was lightened to a mousy blond, his muscles giving away his penchant for athletics…on the field and off. Alex Rosedale, my Australian ex-boyfriend, was standing in my shop *in Ireland*. Once, I would've said I loved him, but now I wanted to asphyxiate on my own vomit at the sight of him.

"What the…*cac*," I swore using the Irish word for shit. Was this the Three of Swords manifesting? Had to be.

"Skye," he said, his accent sounding strange to my ears after months of living among the thick Irish spoken in Derrydun.

"How…"

"An old lady over in that pink cafe told me I would find you here," he said.

"Mary," I said, narrowing my eyes. "Her name is Mary."

He shrugged. "Uh, can we talk?"

I glanced at Lucy, who was watching our exchange with curiosity.

"Can you hold the fort for a sec?" I asked. "I won't be long."

When she nodded, I grabbed Alex's arm and practically dragged him out onto the street.

"Ow," he complained as I pulled him away from the shop and down the footpath. "Skye, you're worse than a ruckman with that grip."

"What are you doing here?" I demanded, letting him go.

"Good to see you, too." He rubbed his arm and looked back at the shop. "Do you work there?"

"I own it," I retorted. "How did you even know I was here?"

"You changed your hometown on your social media profile."

I rolled my eyes. *Moron.*

"Skye, you just disappeared and never came back. Everyone was worried about you."

"Yeah, right." I couldn't believe that. All my friends had been his first, and when people broke up, they usually stuck with what they knew. Which meant I was ejected from the circle.

"I'm sorry about your mum," he went on, scratching his head nervously.

"Shit happens."

"Can we go somewhere and have lunch or something? So we can talk."

"I can't leave the shop," I replied. "It's Lucy's first day."

He glanced over my shoulder at Irish Moon and didn't mask his disappointment.

"You never really talked about your mum before," he said. "And now you're living in her house and running her business."

"So?" It came out a little short, but I didn't need to justify myself to him. He was the one who'd dumped me, magical conspiracy or not.

"So?" His eyebrows rose. "It's a little left of center for you."

"I needed a fresh start," I replied with a sullen shrug. "After being handed a redundancy and dumped, the last thing I needed was to rot in Melbourne."

"*Ouch.*"

"You're hurt?" I raised my eyebrows. "*Sheesh.*"

Not able to look at him anymore, I turned my gaze to Molly McCreedy's where I saw Maggie out the front. She waved when she saw me and began to walk toward us. *Great.*

I was usually glad to see the Irish bartender, we'd become great friends, but having Alex standing here being argumentative about our breakup—and why was he here, anyway?—wasn't good for my psyche. I would have to explain who he was, and I didn't want to do that, not with the way the Derrydun gossip mill operated.

"Hey," she said, standing beside us. "I just wanted to know if you and Boone..." She trailed off and stared at Alex. "Who's this?"

"This is Alex," I said, glaring at my stupid ex-boyfriend. "He's a…um…*friend* from home."

"Friend?" His lip curled.

Like a beacon of hope, a giant gold coach appeared around the corner, passed us, and began navigating around the hawthorn. Forget saved by the bell, I was saved from further awkwardness by the bus.

"I've got to get back to work," I said, pointing at the coach.

Alex scowled, clearly aware I was pushing him away. "Well, can we talk later?"

"Sure, whatever."

Thankfully, he chose to walk away, and Maggie and I watched him move down the footpath and cross the street before he disappeared behind Mary's Teahouse where the car park was.

Thoroughly annoyed, anxious, and on tenterhooks with my temper, I turned to storm back into Irish Moon, but Maggie caught my arm before I escaped inside.

"That's your ex? What's he doin' here of all places?"

"Hell if I know," I muttered, desperate to get away.

"Does Boone know?"

"No! Alex just showed up now. I didn't know he was coming. I'd forgotten all about him, like an epic bitch."

Maggie gave me a pointed look that said everything. Men didn't usually show up in tiny villages in foreign countries on the other side of the world looking for their ex-girlfriends unless they wanted something. Like getting back together.

"No!" I exclaimed. "*No way.*"

"Just watch out, is all I'm sayin'." Maggie shrugged and started to walk away as the bus began to offload its cargo of cashed-up tourists. "Who ended it?"

"He did!" I wanted to stamp my foot like a pouty toddler who wasn't allowed any more chocolate.

Maggie let out a slow whistle.

Rolling my eyes, I bolted back into the shop where Lucy was readying herself for her first wave of tourists to hit the floorboards.

Alex, here in Derrydun? He couldn't have shown up at a worse time. Things were awkward with Boone and me, I had a business to run, and that wasn't even mentioning the whole witch destiny thing. Alex just didn't fit in my life anymore. My feelings had changed…hadn't they?

Ugh, Maggie was right. Boone was going to hit the roof.

This was trouble. Big trouble.

CHAPTER 4

The Three of Swords was haunting my every step.

From morning to lunch, I sweated it out, knowing it was only a matter of time before Maggie said something to someone, and then that someone said something to someone else… Soon, the entire village would know my ex-boyfriend had turned up, long before I had a chance to tell Boone.

Who needed the Internet when Derrydun had a perfectly adequate phone tree.

By mid-afternoon, there were rustlings on the grapevine, and by close of business, word on the street was things were rocky between Boone and I. At some point, there'd be a fight to the death between the two men. Pistols at thirty paces down the main road.

The only thing that had gone well today was Lucy. She'd taken to selling crystals and souvenirs to tourists like a duck to water. At least I didn't have to worry about the shop. When closing came, I sent her off home and locked up Irish Moon, not knowing what I would find when I went back to the cottage. Happy Boone or mad Boone.

Shuffling around the corner, I took my time, trying to think of a way to let him know he shouldn't be threatened.

There was one thing I didn't understand. If part of my legacy calling me home was dismantling my life so I was free to return, then why was Alex showing up now? It was all a little convenient if you asked me. I'd unlocked my true powers when I'd fought the craglorn and released a golden light that blinded even me, and now here was Alex, bright-eyed and bushy-tailed, wanting who knew what.

Boone was waiting for me when I got home. He was sitting at the kitchen table, leafing through the newspaper like he wasn't a shapeshifter, and I wasn't a witch. It was a picture of normalcy that was odd to my eyes. I almost wished he was still hanging around as Buddy the tabby cat rather than sitting in my house as a man I was about to piss off.

As I walked into the kitchen, he stood and pulled me in for a hug, burying his nose into my hair.

"Hey," he whispered, clearly worked up about something. "Listen, about last night…"

Oh, God, he was going to get all sickly sweet and deep and meaningful about that lamb sandwich before I had the chance to tell him about Alex. *Not good.*

Boone was so sweet, *hot*, and my one and only confidant in this crazy new world, and now I had to tell him Alex had made some kind of grand gesture and was sniffing around. Alex, the man I almost fell in love with before my Crescent legacy had conspired to break us apart.

"Uh…" I pulled back nervously. "There's something I have to tell you…"

His eyes narrowed, and his grip loosened. "What did you do?"

"What did I do?" I scoffed. "*Pfft.*" I extracted myself from his arms. "I didn't do anything, just so you know."

"Then what's happened?"

I wasn't sure there was an easy way of telling him another man was trying to cut his grass, because what other reason was that Australian buffoon here for?

"Alex showed up today."

Boone tensed. "Alex, as in…"

"My ex-boyfriend." I winced, waiting for the explosion.

"Your…" Boone's face began to redden, and I wondered if I should dive under the table for some cover. "What is he doin' here?"

"I don't know!" I pouted, crossing my arms over my chest. "I was busy… I…" I was being totally *lame*.

Boone wasn't convinced I didn't have anything to do with it, though. "Why does any man cross the world to look up their ex-girlfriend?"

"Well, he came a long way for nothing!"

"Are you sure?"

"What do you mean by that?!" I cried, my voice becoming shriller by the second.

"I know things have been—"

A knock at the door silenced out argument but not for long. Boone glanced in the direction of the sound, his lip curling. *Uh, oh.* I began to mull over the shapes I knew he could form—fox, gyrfalcon, tabby cat, horse—and an image of Alex being mauled by a house cat came to mind. It wasn't quite as hilarious as it sounded.

"Is that him?" Boone demanded.

"I…" It probably was, which wasn't going to help anything.

His scowl deepened, and he strode toward the front door.

"*Boone!*"

He wrenched it open, revealing a startled Alex on the other side.

"Are you him?" he demanded. "Are you Alex?"

"Yeah…"

"If you've come here to win Skye back, you can forget about it," Boone practically roared. "She's with me now."

The fan was spinning at high velocity, and the *cac* was being readied for a full force splatter.

"Boone," I said, pulling at his shirt sleeve. I could feel a crackle in the air that had everything to do with his shapeshifter power. "*Calm down.*"

"*Gabh suas ort féin!*" he exclaimed in Irish. I didn't know what it meant, but it didn't sound good.

"Well, this escalated quickly," I drawled.

Stepping in front of Boone, who was a hairsbreadth from changing into a fearsome beast and eating Alex for dinner, I smiled sweetly at my ex. "Will you just give us a moment?"

Alex shrugged and backed away. "Uh, sure?"

Slamming the door closed, I turned on Boone and slapped him on the arm, adding a little Crescent whoop-ass for good measure. My palm connected, and my magic zapped, causing him to flinch in pain.

"Ow!" he exclaimed.

"What's gotten into you?" I demanded.

"What can I say? I'm an *animal.*"

"Boone, I'm with you, okay? What you and I have is nothing like the relationship Alex and I had. It has nothing to do with magic and everything to do with who you are. And this moody moron isn't you!"

He pouted—which was a rather sexy look on him—and ran his hands through my hair.

"What's happening to us?" I whispered. "It wasn't supposed to be like this."

"Aye…" His grip tightened, and he went in for a chaste kiss.

"Let me talk to Alex, okay? He might be a dolt, but he's a decent guy."

"Even though he broke up with you?"

"I don't even know how much of it was voluntary," I mused. "I mean, my life fell apart for a reason…"

Boone's expression darkened, and I realized I'd voiced the wrong concern. He probably thought this was my chance to run off and pick up where I left off. I never expected to be a witch, after all.

"Seriously? *Cúl tóna*," I exclaimed, much to his horror. "Yeah. I learned a few swear words from Maggie."

"Skye…"

"Don't Skye me!"

Wrenching open the door, I stormed outside. Boone was being a complete ass by jumping to the worst possible conclusion. Even if Alex wanted to win me back, it didn't mean I was going to fall for it. Life had changed irrevocably, and I couldn't go back even if I wanted to. The point was, *I didn't want to go back.*

Alex was waiting in the garden, scuffing his toe around the edges of the garden bed. I was getting better at sensing magic, and when I looked at him, I couldn't feel anything. Not even a twang in my heart or my nether regions. Whatever feelings I'd had for him had disappeared in the wake of meeting Boone.

"Hey," he said as I approached.

"Sorry about that," I replied. "I didn't realize he was such a jealous guy."

"Be careful with him, Skye. You know what they say about guys like that."

I resisted the urge to roll my eyes because Boone wasn't like that. Was he? I began to doubt because his behavior was completely out of character, and I hated myself for it. He was the last person I should be worried about even with his amnesia and unknown past.

"Let's walk," I said, leading him away from the cottage and along the path through the edges of the forest.

The little woodland area ran all the way up the hill to the tower house and then fanned out to a full-on thicket that stretched for miles. Also within was the ancient hawthorn tree that was the home of the Crescent Witches for centuries. When I first walked here, I used to be afraid of eyes watching from the darkness, and I would jump a mile at the unknown sounds, but now I didn't fear this place. Not one bit.

The sun was beginning to lower, the sky darkening into twilight. Summer was over, so the days were much shorter, and the temperature was plummeting. In a few months, I was sure I would have my first taste of snow. I was kind of looking forward to building a snowman like they did in Christmas movies. With a carrot nose and everything.

"You've changed," Alex said as we wandered along the path.

"I have?"

"Yeah, you're more… Confident. Older."

I snorted. "Thanks a lot. I'm not even thirty, you know."

"That's not what I meant," he said with a chuckle.

"Hashtag adulting."

"Yeah, exactly."

We fell into an uneasy silence, which was unusual for

us. We'd always been best of friends, in the way friends went out and had a blast together. We would go out three nights a week, seeing live music, going to the movies, a show, the pub, festivals—you name it. We were that social couple who spent more time with other people than alone with each other. I was more likely to pinpoint our relationship ending because of that than any magical meddling.

But in saying that, I'd gotten over our split quickly. I'd had Aileen's death to worry about and everything else, so realistically, I hadn't had time to wallow.

"Alex?"

"Yeah?"

"Why are you here? Really?" I glanced at him expectantly.

He grimaced and shrugged. "I'm not sure anymore."

"Huh?"

"I mean, seeing that guy… I didn't know you'd moved on let alone moved to Ireland."

"We broke up, Alex."

"It's just… You never talked about your family. I didn't know your dad or that your mum was Irish."

"I never knew Aileen," I countered. "She left when I was two, and I don't even remember what she looked like. And my dad, well, you can't help cancer."

"But you still decided to pick up her life and live it," he said, sounding rather annoyed.

"So?" I spat. "It's my choice. I came here not knowing what I would find…"

"You found that guy."

"Oh, no, you don't," I exclaimed, turning to face him. "Don't blame me for our break up. You're forgetting something really important. You're the one who ended it."

I wasn't sure I could blame him for that, knowing what I knew now, but there was no way I was letting him turn me into the bad guy. "What I chose to do after is my, and no one else's, business."

"Skye, it's just completely out of character. You up and left with zero notice and never came back."

"So you said."

I was beginning to wonder if his arrival was yet another magical conspiracy in play. A trick conceived by Carman to sow the seeds of doubt between Boone and me to undermine my strength. I'd hardly begun to explore my magic, so I wasn't sure I was that much of a threat to a thousand-year-old witch. *Pfft*, I didn't even know what she looked like let alone how to battle her. Maybe I could strike her down with my sass.

"Is this where you want to be now?"

I glanced at Alex and shrugged. "I kinda like it. At first, I didn't want to be here because of my mum. She'd dropped me into it, you know? A house and a business on the ass cheek of Ireland, but the people here are really nice, and the shop brings in good money. In Australia… My dad has been gone a long time now, I was handed a redundancy and couldn't find another job, and… Everything fell apart. It's just…"

"A fresh start."

"Yeah." I nodded. "I still have Dad's beach house, though."

"So a reason to come back." He smiled, clearly thinking there was a chance.

There was something that hadn't occurred to me. What happened after the battle to end all battles? What if it never came in my lifetime? What if I were eighty and with a walking frame when I stood on the frontline against Carman? I would have to rock up on my mobility scooter with a crocheted rug over my knee to save Ireland's magical people from annihilation. Good luck with that.

The more I thought about it, the more I wasn't sure what my future held anymore. My destiny was with the Crescents…or was it? Was I bound completely to the survival of magic, or did I have a choice? What if there were no more of us left? Would some other coven step up and take the baton and fight Carman? I didn't even know if there were any other witches out there.

As far as I knew, I was alone in this. Alone and without anyone else but Boone to confide in. Robert O'Keefe, the leprechaun lawyer, didn't count because he'd disappeared over the rainbow after Aileen's funeral and hadn't come back.

Alex represented a normal life. One without fear of death or monsters.

Boone, on the other hand, was part of the life that wanted to kill me.

That was the choice Alex's reappearance had thrown in front of me, for better or worse.

"So how long are you staying here?" I asked.

"Dunno. Depends. Is your boyfriend going to chase me out of town with a pitchfork?"

"For your information, he might work on a farm, but he's not a yokel."

Alex snickered, clearly not impressed. He was a city person, so it wasn't any surprise when he didn't understand.

Returning to the main street, I saw Sean McKinnon lingering outside of Molly McCreedy's and held Alex back. The last thing I needed was for Sean to see us together and start ranting. When he went into the pub, I moved off again.

"So what's so special about this town?" Alex asked as we passed the handicrafts store. "And why is there a tree growing in the middle of the road?"

"That's a hawthorn," I said. "It's a sacred tree here. They're said to guard the doorways into the realm of the fair folk."

"The fair who?"

"Fairies," I replied. "The Irish can be superstitious, so they won't cut down a hawthorn tree, no matter where it grows."

"But in the middle of the road?"

"Even in the middle of the road."

I pointed out the various stores and locals as we walked the length of the village center. "There's Mary's Teahouse, which is owned by Mary Donnelly, a lovely old lady who makes the best scones with clotted cream you'll ever taste. That's the pub, Molly McCreedy's. It's covered in Virginia creeper and dates back hundreds of years. Up the street is a little service station, and see those traffic lights? No one ever pays any attention to them. Red, green, whatever."

"There's never any accidents?"

"Not that I've seen. The drivers here are mental, but they know courtesy." Pointing to the coach bay, I continued, "There's a pretty stream down behind the car park, and see that low fence just there? That's where Fergus sits with his dog and donkey, weaving crosses of St. Brigid out of rushes for the tourists. His dog sits on the donkey's back. You would never believe the amount of money he rakes in even if I told you."

"A dog riding a donkey?" Alex scratched his head,

looking bewildered. "This place sure does sound…interesting."

"There's a ruined tower house up on the hill that was supposedly where one of my ancestors lived." I pointed over the top of Irish Moon where the top of the tower could be spotted over the trees even though the sun was almost completely set by now. "It dates back at least five hundred years."

"Cool." He scuffed his toe against the crack in the footpath. "So…you're happy here?"

I shrugged. I had a lot on my plate I couldn't talk about, but I suppose I was happy enough.

"You sounded happy just now, talking about the donkey and the ruins and the traffic lights."

"Alex…"

"I'm going to stick around for a few days," he declared. "Get to know this place, boyfriend be damned."

"Boyfriend be damned?" I repeated, making a face.

"If you want to stay here, then I'm going to make sure it's right for you." He glanced up at the sky, then checked his watch. "It's getting late. You'd better go home to checkers."

"Checkers?" I snorted, knowing he was taking a dig at Boone's choice of shirt. Red and black checks were his, but not Alex's, thing. "I wouldn't call him that to his face."

"I know. I get the feeling he might punch mine in."

I wasn't going to argue with that. I'd never seen Boone's face that shade of red before.

"Don't let me keep you here," I said in an attempt to discourage him.

"See you tomorrow, Skye." He gave me a little wave and practically skipped over the street to where a lone car was parked by Mary's Teahouse.

Knowing trouble was brewing and not comforted by the fact that magic had nothing to do with it, I legged it down the street and disappeared around the back of Irish Moon.

But when I got back to the cottage, Boone wasn't there.

CHAPTER 5

It was a somber mood at Molly McCreedy's the next night.

After an entire day at the shop with no visit from Boone, I went to have a drink to drown my sorrows, but mostly I went so I could get a decent meal in lieu of the Iron Chef's disappearance.

I was sitting at the bar, picking at the remaining chips on my plate, when someone sat next to me. Assuming it was Sean McKinnon, whose favorite pastime was riling me up whenever I was there, I turned to give him a piece of my mind but found Alex instead.

"Hey," he said like nothing was amiss. "I drove over to Sligo today. There's some good food over that way, and I saw their football team practicing. I've never been into soccer, but it was cool to watch them run through their drills. Hey, have you tried Guinness before? Man, that's a complicated drink. You need to be a rocket scientist to pour a pint."

"No one drinks Guinness here just like no one drinks Fosters back home."

When he realized I was glaring at him, he paused. "What?"

"Don't 'what' me," I retorted.

"Bad day?"

"You're seriously asking me if I had a bad day?" I wanted to slap him one, but he knew exactly what he was doing. Alex might be a 'good guy,' but he knew how to work a situation to his advantage. Playing dumb was one of his go-to tactics.

"Yeah?"

"Everyone knows why you're here," I declared. "The whole village is talking about how you want to win me back. You want to know whose side they're on? *It's not yours.*" And it wasn't mine. Even though the villagers had accepted me into their weird and colorful world, they would still choose Boone over me any day of the week and twice on Sundays.

He glanced around the pub and shrugged.

"I went to Mary's for breakfast this morning, and she gave me a speech about fool men like you. Then I ran into Roy from the farm just outside of the village, who told me this crazy story about a bull and a heifer that was slightly offensive if you ask me. Then Father O'Donegal started reading me bible versus when I went to get lunch. *And* Mrs. Boyle brandished her broomstick at me menacingly as I walked back to the shop! I thought she was going to whack me over the head with it!"

Alex listened to my tirade with a smirk on his face. "Who's Mrs. Boyle?"

"Who's…" I made a face. "She's the menace of Main Street! She'll chase you for a mile if you give her half a chance! Usually, her main target is school children, but she wanted a bigger fish to fry today, thanks to you."

"You know, if you wanted me to, I would move here," he said, keeping his voice low. "If that's what you wanted."

I dropped the chip I'd just picked up and stared at him. "Have you hit your head or something?"

"Skye, I made a mistake…"

This was not happening. This had better not be one of those power of three law things I saw in that TV show *Charmed*. What you put out comes back at you times three. Was that a real-life witch thing? Oh, shit, the *Three* of Swords! The universe was going to serve me three awful cans full of middle-finger salutes. That was what the card was warning me about.

"Hey!"

My heart leaped at the sound Boone's voice behind us. I turned, hoping he hadn't heard the last thing Alex had said to me, but from the look of pure anger on his rugged Irish face, I had more chance of seeing a pig fly backward and upside down singing 'Kumbaya' while doing laps around a campfire.

"Boone," I said, sliding off the stool. "Let me explain…"

"Explain what?" he asked, glaring at Alex, who'd stood beside me. "I heard plenty."

"I don't know why you bother with this guy, Skye. Since I arrived, all I've ever seen him do is disrespect you. You deserve better." He grasped my arm to get my attention. "Let me make it up to you, and you'll see. I should never have let you go."

"You're mad!" I exclaimed. "I said no, Alex."

"I should've taken bets," Sean McKinnon declared from the other end of the bar. "Two to one for Boone."

"*Shut up!*" I screeched at him.

"*Bualfidh mé an cac asat!*" Boone exclaimed, glaring daggers at Alex.

"What does that mean?" I cried.

"It means he's goin' to kick his ass," Sean replied. "Two to one for the Irish."

Like the farmer had shouted the word *go*, Boone launched himself at Alex, fists flying. His knuckles smacked into my ex's face with a *crack*, and my mouth fell open in shock as I stumbled out of the way, my plate of remaining chips forgotten.

Alex's head snapped to the side, but he recovered quickly. Before Boone could duck, he was punched in the nose, then Alex rammed his shoulder into his guts, and they fell to the ground, sending a table and chairs flying. They began wrestling, both their faces red with anger as they tried to get shots in.

I'd never seen Boone raise his hand to anyone other than the craglorn and the wolf, and it was shocking to see him brawling with my ex-boyfriend. Alex I'd seen get into punch-ups on the footy oval but not bar fights, and especially, not over me. I wasn't that special! I was just a smart-mouthed witch with a crystal shop on the ass cheek of Ireland, not some bloody supermodel siren with a trust fund and a private plane. *That* I could believe.

"*Stop it!*" I yelled. "Get off…" I kicked Boone up the ass, but he didn't seem to notice.

"Stand back, Skye," Sean declared. "I'll help you!"

The farmer wobbled over to the thrashing men, stood over the pair, and tipped his beer all over them. The liquid hit, but it did nothing to stop the fight.

"What did you think half a pint of beer was going to do?" I exclaimed.

He shrugged and went on watching the pair with amusement. "I told you. Two to one!"

I flailed helplessly, not sure what to do. No one else was stepping up to break the two morons apart before they tore the pub to shreds. Boone was on top with his fist about to slam into Alex's eye when I felt a telltale buzz in the air. *Magic.* Boone was using his magic to get the upper hand. *I couldn't believe him!*

Reaching behind the bar, I found the hose Maggie used to make drinks with. The one with carbonated water. Pointing it at the two men, I fired. There wasn't much oomph behind the jet of water, but it did the trick.

Soaking the pair of buffoons within an inch of their lives, they broke apart, cursing loudly. Boone in Irish, and Alex in plain old English.

"Stop it!" I yelled, dropping the hose. "You're fighting like children!" Shoving Alex away, I grabbed Boone's arm and began dragging him away. "*Get outside.*"

"*Oh*, he's in trouble," Sean said with glee. "*Um ah!*"

Shoving the door open, I towed Boone out into the night, closing off the commotion inside Molly McCreedy's. Dragging him all the way underneath the hawthorn in the middle of the road, I began blasting him.

"I can't believe you! You used your power against him!"

Boone's scowl deepened, and he glanced away, rubbing the back of his hand over his bloodied nose.

"He might be a dick, but he's still a human. *You fought dirty.*"

"He's musclin' in on you!"

"And I told him no!" I said, seething and seeing a healthy dose of red. "You're always telling me off for using my magic away from the hawthorns. *Only under the branches,* you say! *Not one inch outside or you'll attract a craglorn*, you say! And what do you do?"

"Our magic doesn't work the same way," he argued. "I'm not as powerful as you."

"Seriously? You want to measure the size of our magical dicks now? Is that what this is really about?"

"No!" he shouted. "It's about him stealin' you away from me!"

"So you punch him in the face with your magic?" I snorted. "That's not the point, and you know it. You were one step away from changing completely, weren't you?"

He glared and crossed his arms over his chest.

"Ugh," I declared, throwing my hands up into the air. "By the way, I said *cock* sandwich the other night. Cock as in dick. More specifically, *yours*."

He paled before pouting and turning away.

"I can't even look at you," I said, roaring in frustration.

"Then don't," he snapped, turning on his heel.

"Boone!" I called out as he strode away into the darkness.

He didn't listen. Powering right past Molly McCreedy's, he disappeared around the back where a moment later, I caught a flash of white taking off into the sky.

Typical. He'd flown away rather than take responsibility for his actions. There was more going on here than just Alex, but hell, if I knew, when he wouldn't tell me.

Walking back to the pub, I leaned against the wall and seethed, not quite ready to go inside and face the destruction. What was happening to us? We were supposed to be a team. We'd saved each other's lives…

The light overhead dulled the street around me, making the night even darker. The only thing I had to fear around here were magical creatures looking for a feed, but I was aware of those things more and more, so I wasn't bothered. Wasn't it ironic that, as it turned out, it was humans I had to be wary of?

The door opened, revealing a disheveled Alex, and I rolled my eyes. Being stuck in the middle was the worst. Was this one of those annoying love triangles? Unlikely, I would have to want both men for our powers to combine or some stupid thing.

"I'm sorry," Alex said sheepishly. "I shouldn't have egged him on like that."

Narrowing my eyes, I retorted, "No, you shouldn't have."

"You're right about one thing."

"What's that?"

"This town is nuts." He laughed, not bothered he'd gotten into a fight at all.

"You're going to have a black eye," I declared out of spite.

"A real shiner."

"*Good.*"

This was becoming a real pain in my backside. Alex being here had been a real blast from the past, but he just wasn't getting it. We were over, and nothing he or I did could turn back the dial and bring my mother back from the dead. That was the only way I would be free of the Crescents and able to live my own life. The problem with that was I didn't want to go back. Not after seeing the things I'd seen, and especially, not after knowing Boone. Not the Boone from tonight, the Boone who'd pledged himself to the Crescent Witches. The Boone who'd kissed me by that spring after saving my life. The Boone who'd given me his heart.

"Alex, it's nice to see you and everything, but I'm with Boone now."

"Yeah, I can see that."

I sighed, hoping he would take the hint and back down for all our sakes. Nothing was going to change even if I wanted it to. Which I didn't.

"But that's just for now," he said with a wicked smile.

"Alex…"

"Oh, and don't worry about cleaning up inside. I took care of it. Unlike your boyfriend, who just left you standing out here in the dark on your own." He rolled his eyes. "He's a real catch, Williams."

"Don't talk to me like I'm one of your football buddies."

"You know, that's what I love about you most, Skye. You don't bullshit. You just say it like it is."

I tensed at the word love. "You should go home, Alex. Go home, and find some nice girl who you don't have to fruitlessly convince to love you. How's that for telling it like it is?"

He smiled, my barb bouncing right off him. "I'm not ready to give up on us yet. We were amazing together. I'm sorry, I let you go, and I promise to make it up to you. You can trust me again, Skye. You'll see."

Leaning against the wall with a groan as he sauntered off into the night to find his car, I cursed the day the Crescents called me home. This wasn't in the witchy handbook. Not one scrap.

I continued to sulk on my own, but Maggie appeared, forcing me to wipe the sullen expression off my face.

"Skye! What the bleepin' hell is goin' on?" she exclaimed. "I go on me break for ten minutes, and the place falls apart. Then Sean tells me Boone punched that Australian moron in the face?"

"If anything's broken, I'll get it fixed." I snorted and rubbed my eyes, not giving a stuff if I smeared my mascara.

"Don't worry about that," she said, waving her hand at me. "What about you? You don't still love him do you?"

"Who? Alex? *No!*" I immediately fired back. "It never got to that point! He dumped me, remember?"

"Seems like he thinks he's made a mistake. What about Boone?"

"He's stormed off someplace," I said, beginning to feel exhausted by all the drama. "I want him, Maggie. Only him, but something isn't right. It's not Alex… It's something else."

"Then you need to talk to him about it."

"It's like beating my head against a brick wall… *Speaking of.*" I turned to face the wall, braced my hands against the whitewashed walls and reared my head back.

"Don't do that," Maggie said, tugging me away. "You'll give yourself a blindin' headache."

"I don't know what else to do."

"Go home to bed," she said kindly. "Let those fools sulk for the night, and tomorrow, go find Boone and talk to him." There was a crash inside, and she groaned. "That'll be Sean 'helping' right the tables." She air quoted and rolled her eyes. "I better go back inside, or he'll make the mess worse."

"I thought Alex…" I frowned.

"Aye, he mopped the floor." She shooed me away. "Off with you. I'll call you tomorrow, and, Skye? Don't worry about anythin'. Boone's sulkin' now, but I see the way he looks at you, and I see the way you look at him. You'll work it out."

Watching her disappear into the pub and begin shrieking at Sean, I hoped she was right.

I didn't know what I would do without Boone.

CHAPTER 6

The next morning dawned, and like the weather knew my heart was melancholy, a thick fog clung to the landscape.

Summer was well and truly over now. The days were shorter, and a chill was beginning to seep into the country air, signaling autumn had well and truly taken hold. Leaves were turning bright shades of yellow, orange, and red, falling from branches and littering the ground. School kids kicked piles of them into the air as they ran for the bus at the end of the main road, vexing Mrs. Boyle no end. Considering her broom had morphed into a rake, they should have been in fear for their lives, but were faster on their feet than the old woman was.

It was a short walk from my cottage to Irish Moon, but I still didn't chance it without a jacket. Today, it didn't help to keep the cold away, and I shivered as I made the trek to work.

Rounding the corner onto the main road, I skidded to a halt when I almost smacked into Sean McKinnon. He was standing just around the corner, and when he glared like I'd kicked his kitten, I knew he'd been waiting to see me. I was about to cop an earful…and to think I'd used my power to calm his aching heart that night I found him drunk in the gutter outside Molly McCreedy's! Even if I weren't aware I'd been doing it, I would never do it again.

I looked over his messy hair, flannel shirt, and dirty-at-the-knees jeans and scowled.

"Have at it then," I drawled. "Give me a piece of your addled mind."

"Boone's miserable, and it's all your fault," he declared. "He was perfectly happy before *you* came along. You ruined him."

I gasped dramatically. "Take that back!"

"No! I can't! You're the witch who led him on and broke his heart!" Sean thumped his chest. "I know a man in pain when I see one. *Is gan í bheith.*"

"What does that mean?" I demanded, feeling my face turn red in annoyance.

"Forlorn," Sean stated, puffing out his chest.

Forlorn… My heart twisted as the word conjured up an image of the craglorn. *The ravaged and the lonely.*

"You leave him alone, Skye Williams," he went on. "Or else."

"Or else what?" I pouted and stared him down, not afraid of Sean McKinnon, the town drunk. He was a drunk because he hadn't managed to get over the death of his wife, Juliette, so it was mean of me to insult him like that, but I was angry. No one had any idea what Boone and I shared. *No one.*

"You'll see," he said mysteriously, then ambled off like he hadn't just threatened me with a pox on my house.

My mouth fell open, and I bristled with rage as he wandered down the footpath and climbed into his little red

Toyota—the car Boone and I had borrowed for our journey to Croagh Patrick months ago—and revved the engine like a hooligan.

There were footsteps behind me, and I glanced over my shoulder to see Lucy had arrived just in time to catch the last of Sean's spectacular one-sided argument.

"What happened?" she asked, watching Sean spin his tires and roar down the road toward Roy's farm.

"Boone got into a fist fight with Alex at the pub last night. Sean is all bent over it."

"Seriously?" Her eyes widened. "Two hot men were fighting over you?"

"It's not as cool as it sounds," I said, turning to unlock the shop. "At this point, I'm about ready to hand them over to someone else. You can have them if you want."

"Why is Sean gettin' involved?"

"Sean and Boone are best mates," I explained. "They couldn't be any more different, but for some reason only they know, they're buddies."

Opening the door, I held it ajar for Lucy, and she stepped inside.

"They say opposites attract," she offered.

"I'll say."

"Things are still shaky with you two?"

I nodded and thought about the Three of Swords, my heart stinging with matching phantom stab wounds.

"It'll work out," Lucy offered kindly. "Life always goes in ebbs and flows. Maybe you can draw another tarot card?"

"Maybe," I replied, turning on the lights.

As we settled into our routine for the day, Lucy following the list Mairead had written in her employee handbook, I sat behind the counter and shuffled my tarot cards. Drawing a card from the top, I narrowed my eyes when I saw my old buddy the Three of Swords rear its ugly head. Shuffling again, I drew from the middle of the deck just to confuse the universe, but it was too smart for a newbie like me. The Three of Swords appeared again.

Just like that, I knew this was no momentary bump in the road of life. It was a *chasm* so dark and deep there was no bottom in sight. Three swords would pierce my heart before this was over. Three, painful, sharp swords. In one side, and out the other.

I didn't see Boone all day, and he didn't come over that night, either. He didn't even show his face as Buddy, the tabby cat.

As I watched a frozen meal rotate in the microwave, I pushed away a pang of loneliness. This place wasn't the same without him.

The next day, I didn't open Irish Moon. It was a Sunday, and I didn't fancy working seven days a week, not when I felt so rotten.

The ancient hawthorn towered over me, her limbs sheltering me from the world. Sitting in a hollow at the base of the trunk, I ran my fingers along the bark, tracing the lines of her snarled roots.

Everything was so messed up. I'd thought things were supposed to get better now I was beginning to understand this whole witch business, but it only seemed to be growing worse. Boone was the only person I could confide in, and he'd pushed me away.

Fiddling with the crystal hanging around my neck, I felt out the edges of my magic. Closing my eyes, I imagined a golden ball of light inside my chest. Boone said this was how I chose to manifest my power, that this was my own personal way of connecting so I could bring it forth into the world. I supposed it meant it was different for every witch, but I wouldn't know. I didn't know any other witches.

At the thought of Boone, I swallowed the lump in my throat. Without him…

I needed help. I wasn't too proud to admit it, especially when I had the fate of magic breathing down the back of my neck. There was no way I was choking. One day, I would be able to use my magic freely and without fear, but it was up to me.

Fisting my hands into my hair, I sucked in a sharp breath. What had I ever achieved other than third place in an egg and spoon race at Primary School? Maybe a gold star on my English homework, but that was about it. Now I was meant to be some sort of messiah. *Lucky Ireland.*

The sound of footsteps crunching on leaf litter and the rustling of ferns brushing against shins drew my attention, and I glanced up.

I stood, severing the contact I'd made with my magic, and my heart leaped as I saw Boone emerge out of the forest.

His face bore no marks from the fight with Alex on Friday night, but I knew he would come out of it without a scratch. Especially when his shapeshifter genes contributed to accelerated healing.

"Boone! Where have you been?" I asked, hoping this was the moment we would work everything out.

"Workin'," he said.

An uneasy silence fell, the sound of the forest the only thing that passed between us.

"Skye, listen…"

No speech beginning with '*Skye, listen*' ended well. Not a single one.

"It's always been so easy with us," I blurted, desperate to get in first. "We would joke, flirt, and talk… Ever since we kissed by the spring at Croagh Patrick… Then… Then after the craglorn…" I fought back tears. "It's been awkward ever since."

He cast his gaze away, which didn't help one bit.

"What did I do?" I asked desperately. "What's so wrong with me?"

"Nothin'…" he muttered. "Don't worry about it."

"I will worry about it!" I stepped forward, grasped his stupid red and black checkered shirt, and practically shook him. "What's going on with you? It's like… It's like you regret kissing me."

The words stung as I blurted them out, but it was the root of my fear. Alex showing up had just amplified all of our problems like salt in an open wound.

Boone looked as if I'd stabbed him right through the heart.

"Boone, I can't help if you won't talk to me!" I exclaimed.

"Alex…" he began.

"I don't want him!"

"You were so concerned Lucy might be a fae, yet you never stopped to think about Alex's motives for bein' here, did you?"

"What does that mean?" I froze, my heart jackhammering wildly in my chest. "You think he's… *No.* I would know. He knows things…" I shook my head. "That's not the point. I'm talking about you and me."

He averted his gaze and began prying my fingers away from his shirt.

"Maybe you're right," he murmured. "Maybe we shouldn't have started somethin'. Not if it's goin' to be like this."

"What?" I was numb as his words sunk in. *Was he breaking up with me?* "But… I thought… You said your heart…" I choked on my words as my throat started to burn.

"Me loyalty is still with the Crescents," he said, and that was it. He didn't say any more. He just turned and walked away, leaving me standing in the clearing, too stunned to move let alone shout after him.

I didn't think it was possible to long for someone as much as I did now. Boone was there the day I first arrived in Derrydun and hadn't left my side. He'd taken the shape of Father O'Donegal's tabby cat so he could sneak into the cottage and watch over me. He'd fought the wolf that had attacked me in his fox shape long before I knew it was him, and he'd risked everything by leaving the boundary of the hawthorns that protected him to help me charge the athame to defeat the craglorn.

He'd risked his life again and again for me. Hadn't he? Or was it just because Aileen had saved his life, and he was bound to the Crescents? I didn't want to acknowledge the fact he might only be sticking around because I was the last of the coven. He'd given me his heart the night we'd fought the craglorn. *He'd given it to me.*

"What did I do?" I asked the hawthorn. "I didn't ask for any of this." Pressing my palms against the trunk, I sobbed. "I don't want to be alone… I want Boone…"

The world shifted, and I gasped as images began to flash through my mind. One after the other with no way for me to decipher any of them. Was the hawthorn…*intelligent?*

Pulling my hands away, I gasped, my head spinning. Crumpling to my knees, I sank into the hollow, the magic of the hawthorn unsettling my stomach.

The hawthorn… Was it watching? *Did it know?*

Closing my eyes, I tried to fight off a wave of exhaustion. The fight had hardly begun, and I was already so tired…

"Skye?"

A hand was shaking my shoulder.

"*Skye?*"

My eyes cracked open, and a face came into view.

Lucy.

She was kneeling in front of me, her hair pulled back in a loose plait, the freckles on her cheeks more pronounced than ever. Bright blue feathers hung from her ears, and her floral shirt was topped with a blue denim jacket.

"Are you all right?" She was frowning at me.

I wiped my hands at my eyes, then tried to straighten my hair, which was a tangled mess. I probably had a million leaves stuck in it and maybe a bug or two. Smoothing down my top, I clucked my tongue when I saw my side was covered in dirt. I hoped this wasn't going to become a *thing*. Me falling asleep in odd places.

"What are you doin' out here?" Lucy asked, helping me sit.

"I fought with Boone," I muttered. "And I, uh…" I finished off my rambling explanation with a shrug. I couldn't exactly tell her a magical hawthorn tree showed me a million visions I didn't have a hope of understanding.

"And you fell asleep in the woods?" She raised her

eyebrows but thankfully wasn't patronizing about it. "You're going to catch a cold bein' out here like this."

What was *I* doing out here? What was *she* doing lurking around the hawthorn? Thinking about what Boone said, about being so worried about her magical orientation, my hackles rose. Without thinking, I reached out and grasped her arm, then touched her with my magic.

Immediately, I was zapped with static electricity. I pulled away sharply, not knowing what it meant—if it meant anything at all.

"*Ow*," Lucy exclaimed, shivering.

"Sorry…"

"Good ol' static electricity," she said with a wink. "It gets the best of all of us at some point. Do you want some company on the walk home?"

"What are you doing out here?" I asked, rising to my feet and picking leaves out of my hair.

"Just walkin'," she replied. "I wanted to see the tower house. After seeing it, I wandered down here for a bit, then I found you."

I narrowed my eyes and nodded. What could I say to that?

If she were out here to try to take advantage of my fragile state, you know, being a spy for Carman and all, I would have to take drastic measures. That would be a shame because I kind of liked her and her bohemian attitude. I had to deliver a passive-aggressive thinly veiled warning in lieu of the spell I'd been working on—that wouldn't confuse her if she weren't at all magically inclined —and it was going to suck.

"Lucy, I hope you don't take this the wrong way, but…" I sighed, knowing she would take it like a cat took a thermometer up the bum. "It's just… I don't need another complication right now. Things are messy, I'm still trying to settle, and—"

Lucy made a face and laughed. "Hey, you're me boss. I'm the one who has to impress you. Not the other way around."

I snorted. "I suppose so."

"You want me to walk with you?" she asked again.

"No, it's fine. I don't have far to go."

"Okay, well, I'll see you tomorrow."

I nodded. "See ya."

In all the chaos, I'd forgotten about the spell I'd been working on to verify her magical affiliation. I suppose protecting the magical people of Ireland was still important even when I was the subject of a love triangle.

"Hey, Lucy?" I called out. "Can I have a strand of your hair?"

"Huh?" She turned and waited.

"I said, watch your step over there." *So lame.*

"Oh." She smiled and waved. "Thanks."

I watched her walk away, and the moment she'd left the clearing, I took the opposite path and headed home, my mind swimming. The argument with Boone was still tumbling through my head, and it ached after the strange communion I'd shared with the hawthorn. I knew the tree was full of magic but memories, as well? I suppose it was a possibility considering it was the ancestral home of the Crescent Witches. Still, it freaked me out.

As I walked back toward the village, I felt the presence of the hawthorn subside behind me, and as it did, it took the soothing balm touching its trunk had given me, and loneliness opened up in my heart once more.

CHAPTER 7

S leep didn't come easy that night.

Images flashed through my mind, making it impossible to drift off. My heart ached, my eyes were puffy and full of grit, and the encounter with the hawthorn was really bothering me. I knew I should've been trying to focus on the message it was trying to shove into my brain, but I was too focused on the argument with Boone.

I knew this Crescent Witch thing wasn't supposed to be easy, but I thought I would have him there to help. Maybe I was being selfish. Or maybe I was expecting too much from him. He didn't know much about anything when I took his amnesia into account. All he knew was what Aileen had taught him when he landed in Derrydun almost four years ago.

Rolling over, I glanced at the alarm clock and groaned. The time flicked over to eight a.m. and instantly began to flash as the alarm blared. *Buzz, buzz, buzz, buzz…* Thumping my hand on the top, I silenced the awful racket and rubbed my eyes, trying to remember some of the absurd dreams I'd had.

It was always the same if I coasted on the edge of sleep and wakefulness. My dreams were crazier than a boyfriend who could morph into a fox. The more I tried to remember, the faster I forgot. Was that the definition of ironic? I didn't know, but it sure felt like it.

Dragging myself out of bed and into the shower, I got ready for work in a daze, still feeling miserable after the argument with Boone under the hawthorn. I suspected Lucy, but he suspected Alex. Who was right? Or were we both wrong?

Shuffling outside, I made my way to the main street, my fingers closing around the shop keys in my jacket pocket. *Maybe we shouldn't have started somethin'.* He was so wrong. Boone and I…

The sound of raised voices reached my ears as I stumbled around the corner. It didn't really register in my foggy brain until I saw Lucy and Alex talking heatedly outside Irish Moon. Alex and Lucy. *Lucy and Alex.*

She was scowling at him as he talked, and he was waving his hands wildly. It looked awkward as hell…and completely suss.

Stepping back before they saw me, I peered at them, watching their conversation unfold. Too bad I didn't know a spell to improve my hearing—if such a thing existed. Sometimes, I wish I had a wand to wave and a book of spells with simple commands like in *Harry Potter*. A summer program at Hogwarts would be helpful right about now.

After a moment, I knew he wasn't going away, nor was my burning curiosity, so I strode around the corner, madder than a bee in a jar.

"What are you doing here?" I demanded, jabbing a finger at Alex. "Don't you think you've caused enough pointless drama?"

"You know why I'm here," he replied, turning to face me.

I gasped as I saw the dark blue-black bruise over his left eye, and my hand flew to my mouth. Boone really clocked him one.

"Is it that horrible?" he asked with a chuckle. "It'll go away, you know."

"Oh, go and *vague-book* about it." I made a face, resisting the urge to stick my tongue out at him.

"I've got better things to do than post clickbait on social media," he said with a smirk.

"What's more important than taking a hint?" I muttered, unlocking the door so Lucy and I could escape inside.

Alex sneered, his lip curling at an unattractive angle. The black eye didn't help his chances of not looking like a complete douchebag, either.

"If you don't mind, I've got a business to run," I declared, closing the door in his face.

Turning, I knew full well he was still standing there, staring at me through the glass like a creepy stalker. At one time, his attention would've thrilled me, but now it was overkill. Kill being the word to worry about.

"Wow," Lucy said, turning on the lights. "I never thought small town livin' would be exactly like an episode of *Ballykissangel*."

"Bally-who now?"

"It's a TV show," she explained with a laugh. "It's an Irish drama about the crazy life in a small, remote Irish village. You know, it's got all the classic storylines. Love, scandal, schemes…"

Sounded like Derrydun but without half the stuff that

made it the most insane place on the planet. Just add a secret coven of witches or something like that.

Glancing over my shoulder, I was relieved to see Alex had disappeared. I needed to get it through his thick skull that I wasn't getting back together with him, nor was I leaving Derrydun. We needed to sit down and hash it out, and Boone—wherever he was—wasn't going to like it one bit.

"I'm sorry," I said to Lucy. "You started working here at a really strange time. Everything is ass up…"

"Havin' two men fightin' over you sounds like bliss, but I can see it isn't."

"It's a good plot for a movie," I said with a snort. "Or that TV show of yours. But real life? *Forget about it.*"

"Be careful, Skye," she said, looking worried. "I don't have a good feelin'."

"About?"

She glanced away and began dusting the glass cabinet erratically.

"*Lucy.*"

She paused, holding the feather duster mid-dust, and her cheeks flushed red.

"Lucy," I said again. "What did he say to you?"

"Nothing. He just…" She sighed dramatically. "There was an undertone."

"Undertone of what?"

Lucy turned back to her dusting, moving along to the amethyst cave that was the size of her head. She flicked the feather duster around inside, cleaning the purple crystal teeth.

"*Lucy.*"

"Malice," she said. "There were undertones of malice."

I shivered, the image of the sneer that had carved Alex's face coming to mind. I'd never seen him look like that before. I didn't regret kissing Boone by the spring under Croagh Patrick, but he was beginning to all because of Alex and his unrelenting pursuit of me. He was trying to break us up, and when the moment was right, he would swoop in and be the shoulder I needed to cry on. Well, I had news for him!

"Don't worry about me," I said, taking out the tarot cards from underneath the counter. "I don't intend to let him get anything. I'm not going back."

Shuffling the cards, I drew one from the top and scowled when I saw it was the Three of Swords. *Again.* It was a warning, plain and simple, just like the Tower had been.

"I know I've only been around a few days," Lucy began. "But if you need anything…"

"Thanks. I'll be fine. Don't you worry about Alex. I'll handle him." I rolled my eyes and put the card back into the stack. "This has gone on for far too long if you ask me."

"You're goin' to confront him?" Her eyes bulged.

"Yeah. Looks like it's the only way he's going to get the hint." And I would use magic to suggestively push him back onto a plane back to Australia if I had to. Then there was the Boone factor.

Honestly, I wasn't even sure he'd broken up with me yesterday or if it was just a fight. I had to convince him that he was the only man I wanted, and whatever was going on didn't change what was in my heart one iota.

Whatever Boone was dealing with, I would help him. Not because I was bound by duty but because I cared about him…even when he was sulking.

Glancing out the window, my heart skipped a beat as I saw Boone walking into Mary's Teahouse.

"Lucy?"

"Yeah?" She poked her head out from behind the bookshelf.

"Do you think you'd be okay minding the shop for ten minutes?"

"Sure!" Lucy smiled and nodded enthusiastically. "A chance to prove myself."

Storming out of Irish Moon, I powered across the street toward the neon pink cottage with the thatched roof. Opening the door, I weaved through the tables, a woman on a mission.

"Good mornin', Skye!" Mary said brightly from behind the counter.

Mary Donnelly was a sweet little Irish lady, with a perm and a blue rinse, that loved the color pink and feeding scones and clotted cream to tourists. Apparently, she also had a penchant for spring weddings, which was a problem considering Boone's and my current relationship status.

When I first arrived in Derrydun, her accent was so thick I couldn't understand a single word she said, then one day, it was like someone had turned on a switch inside my head and ever since, she was clear as a bell. I always figured it was a magic thing like someone had implanted a language chip in my brain, but maybe it was a cultural assimilation thing. I'd finally gotten used to the Irish.

"Hi, Mary," I muttered, walking straight past her and into the back where I found Boone stacking boxes.

He glanced up when I appeared, raised an eyebrow, and went straight back to stacking the delivery of flour and molasses—whatever Mary needed *that* for—promptly ignoring me.

"We need to talk," I said.

"We talked yesterday," he said, not even looking at me.

"Boone. That wasn't talking. Not proper talking, anyway."

"Listen," he said, turning to scowl at me. "I understand. Aileen explained it to me in a round about way."

"Explained what?"

"The Crescent…callin'. Or whatever you call it. Destiny tore you away from Alex. Neither of you truly wanted to end things, but you had no choice. Magic screwed up your life and brought you here because of me."

"Shut up!" I exclaimed.

He blinked, stunned by my outburst.

"Shit happens," I went on. "You didn't mean for Aileen to…*die*. That was her choice." I sighed, resisting the urge to roll my eyes. "I didn't know about all this when Alex dumped me, but I'm here now, and I've accepted this is my life. I want it, Boone. Stuff destiny and magical whatever. I choose to be here with you. I choose it regardless of all those things."

He didn't reply, which vexed me even more.

"Look, I'm not dumb, you know. I don't know what's going on with you because there's something that has nothing to do with Alex, but you don't have to worry about me. You don't have to worry about us, you hear? You and me, we're solid. Right?"

Boone snorted and shook his head.

"You don't believe me." My heart sank. Maybe we had broken up after all, and I was just living in denial.

"You have somethin' you need to work out with him,"

he said, turning to finish stacking the pile of boxes. "So go, and work it out. I'll still be here because *I can't leave.*"

"Boone…"

"Don't you have a shop to run? Or have you left your suspected fae in charge?"

I backed away, wanting nothing more than to slap him around the ear. Why were men so pigheaded?

"You'll see," I murmured. "When he goes the hell away, and I'm still here annoying the shite out of you, *you'll see.*"

Spinning on my heel, I strode out of the back room and through the teahouse, much to Mary's puzzlement.

"Skye!" she called out after me. "Skye, dear! How do you like lilies for the centerpieces?"

CHAPTER 8

Staring at the Three of Swords, I felt like tearing it up into little pieces and tossing it into the bin.

Leaning my elbows on the counter at Irish Moon, I squinted at the golden lines of the drawing and tilted it from side to side. Other than the metallic print shimmering in the light, the movement revealed nothing.

"What card is that?" Lucy asked, standing in front of me.

"The Three of Swords." I flipped it over so she could see.

"What does it mean?"

"It means a world of pain, that's what it means."

The bell over the door rang merrily, causing me to glance up, and when I saw who it was, I wished I had a literal sword, not a metaphoric one.

Alex closed the door behind him, and then smiled when his gaze met mine.

"You're unbelievable." I was getting eye strain from all the eye rolling. I wondered at what point that became an actual problem. Would my eye pop right out of my head, and would I have to shove it back in there? I would probably have to wear a funky eye patch like a pirate. Thinking about the time Boone and I dug up the Crescent athame from inside the tower house, I snorted. Boone could turn into a gyrfalcon, but what about a parrot? A rainbow lorikeet… Yeah, he could totally be one of those.

"Skye," Alex began, glancing nervously at Lucy. "We need to talk."

"Yeah, we do," I shot back.

"When?"

I sighed. "After the shop closes. I'll meet you up the hill at the tower house. How's that?"

He smiled, his eyes sparkling. "Great."

"Until then, leave me alone," I said, turning back to my tarot cards.

The bell rang, signaling he'd gone, and I sighed again. I was so over this whole debacle. Alex was going to get smacked down this afternoon, and hopefully, that would be the end of it, and things could go back to normal. Well, as normal as things got in this place, being a witch and all.

Lucy stood beside me as we watched Alex disappear out of view.

"Are you sure you want to go up there alone with him?" she asked.

"I've known him a long time," I replied. "I doubt he's going to hack me up into little pieces and stuff me in a hessian bag."

"Are you sure?"

"Lucy!"

"Just lookin' out for you," she replied with a halfhearted smile.

"You don't have to worry about me," I said, knowing if push came to shove, I would be able to give back ten times as hard with my magic. But I hoped it wouldn't come to that, especially away from the immediate range of the hawthorns. I knew I was protected to a certain extent at the tower house, but my magic was strong. I found that out when I made my talisman in the exact same spot and invited the craglorn over for the all you can eat Crescent Witch buffet.

"He's absolutely convinced," she mused.

"About?" I reached for my talisman and held it tightly, feeling the thread of magic within.

"That it's only a matter of time before you realize what a mistake you've made."

"I haven't made any mistakes," I shot back. "Not about this. People get confused over their hearts all the time, but that's only because they have their cake and want someone else's, too. That's a metaphor for emotional greed, by the way. I'm happy with my *Boone-cake*. He's more than enough for one person, believe me. He's a ten-tiered, chocolate mud cake with buttercream icing, sprinkles, cherries, jam filling, and a spoonful of Nutella on the side. You would think you'd get sick after tasting a cake like that, but not me. Hand me a bigger spoon. *Stat.*"

Lucy chuckled and patted me on the shoulder. "Good for you. Not many people can say they found a cake like that."

"Yeah," I muttered, my heart feeling heavy at the thought of what Boone must be going through right now. "Yeah, I am…"

What a hopeless situation.

***

Alex was waiting for me at the tower house.

Approaching, my boots crunched on the gravel path, and I narrowed my eyes. *Blunt and to the point,* I thought. *Send him packing.*

He was sitting on the wooden fence separating the path from the ruin, his feet swinging back and forth. He didn't stand as I neared, he just stopped his feet and sat patiently. Sitting beside him on the round log, I was careful to leave a healthy amount of space between us. It wasn't exactly a comfortable position, the wood was hard against the bones in my ass cheeks, but it didn't matter. Only my words did.

Alex didn't say hello, but neither did I. I think we were beyond the point of pleasantries.

"You can't come here and expect me to drop everything for you," I said. "It's unrealistic."

"Not if you love someone."

"And I don't love you, Alex. I might've been able to once but not anymore. We had fun together, but I've moved on. You should, too."

He glanced over my shoulder and then back to me. "Well," he said. "Let's see."

Before I could dodge out of the way, he reached out, grasped my face, and planted his lips on mine. When his tongue tried to force its way into my mouth, I flailed my arms and shoved him back.

"Alex…"

"What do you think you're doin'?"

The sound of Boone's voice sent ice sliding through my veins. Alex had set me up!

Rising to my feet, I spun on my heel and came face-to-face with an enraged Boone.

"You saw that!" I exclaimed, jabbing a finger at Alex. "You saw me push him away!"

"I saw you kissin' him." Boone narrowed his eyes, clearly hurt.

"I didn't kiss him," I argued. "I…"

"After everythin' I did for you…" he muttered. "After I…" He snorted, then strode off across the meadow and leaped over the stone fence into the field.

Turning on Alex, I jabbed a finger at him.

"You knew he was standing there!" I shrieked. "I can't believe you!"

"Skye, I said I would fight for you," he said, standing.

"Don't you get it! You lost the day you broke up with me. *You never had a chance.*"

"Skye…"

He stepped forward, his arms rising to capture me in an embrace, but I'd had a gut full of his meddling. How many times had I told him I wasn't interested? I was fairly sure it was about a million by now, so if he wasn't listening to my words, then he sure as hell would listen to my fist.

In a whirlwind of fury, I launched my knuckles at his face, aiming for his good eye. My hand smacked into his eye socket with a satisfying *thwack*, and I winced as the impact jarred up my arm. *Geez, no one told me it hurt to hit someone.*

Shaking my hand, I glared at Alex, who was holding his hands over his eye and staring at me open-mouthed.

"You punched me!" he exclaimed.

"Yeah, and if you don't get the hint, I'll kick you in the balls, too." I backed away, aiming for the direction Boone had gone. "The answer has been the same as it's always been, Alex. N-o. No. No, no, no, no, *no*. I don't love you. I love Boone. The. End."

Turning, I left him standing on top of the hill in the shadow of the tower house and crossed the meadow. My heart span and span, the words echoing around in my head like a stone rattling in a tin can. I'd said the words. *The words.*

I wasn't sure if I should be seething or soaring after what had just happened. My hand was throbbing with a dull ache, and I hoped I'd given Alex another black eye. He desperately needed a matching set.

Attempting a graceful leap over the fence, my foot caught, and I rolled over the stone like a tub of lard and landed on my face in the grass. There went any residual adrenalin I'd gathered from punching that twat in the face.

Scrambling to my feet and hoping no one had seen my commando roll, I legged it over the field. Sheep scattered, bleating in panic as I made my way toward Roy's farm. I wiggled ungracefully over another fence, almost slipped on my ass on the muddy track, and stepped in a pile of animal shite—that I had to stop and scrape off my boot on the fence—before I finally made it to the farmhouse.

The excited barking of Roy's black and white border collie, Phee, erupted as she sensed my presence, and she barreled around the corner and practically leaped into my arms.

"Hey, girl," I said gently, trying to fend off her pink tongue. I'd had enough unwanted French kissing for one day, thank you very much.

"Phee! Down!" There was a sharp whistle, and the dog backed off and ran back toward Roy, who'd follow the excited sheepdog's flight.

"Hey," I said, raising my hand as the old man waddled around the corner.

"Skye. This is a surprise. Is somethin' the matter? Need help towin' a car out of the creek again?"

I groaned, shaking a fist at the sky. The last time I'd

asked Roy for a favor was when the real estate agent I'd called to evaluate Irish Moon for sale had almost smashed into the hawthorn in the middle of the village, swerved to miss, and landed in the creek behind Mary's Teahouse instead. We had to get the farmer and his tractor to pull the poor guy out. Would Derrydun ever let it go?

"I'm looking for Boone," I said. "Is he here?"

"Is somethin' the matter with you two? The lad's been grumpy the last week. Ever since that Australian lad appeared." He narrowed his eyes.

"Give me a break!" I exclaimed. "I just gave him a black eye to match the one Boone gave him."

"You did?"

"Have you seen him or not?"

"Nay," he replied. "He was here today but left a while ago."

I pinched the bridge of my nose. He must've finished work, then crossed the field. It was shorter to visit the sheep than to take the main road back into the village. And there I was sitting by the tower house with Alex, right in his path. Talk about moronic.

"Thanks, anyway," I said, reaching down to scratch Phee behind the ears. "If you see him, can you tell him I stopped by?"

"Aye." Roy nodded.

Heading back the way I came, I fared much better over the fences and dodged all the piles of animal shite. When I passed the tower house, Alex had already left, which was good news for him. I was a hairsbreadth away from sinking my boot into the family jewels and stomping on his grapes.

It was a long shot, but Boone wasn't at the cottage, Mary's Teahouse, or Molly McCreedy's. No one had seen him, either. I stopped by his little cottage on the outskirts the village—the cottage he hadn't let me see—but he wasn't there. He wasn't anywhere.

Not knowing what else to do and way past leaving him alone to wallow, I went to the hawthorn in the woods.

Staring up at the tree, I grasped the talisman around my neck and closed my eyes. Imagining the ball of golden light in my chest, I thought about Boone. *Where are you? Come to me...*

I had no idea if it would work, but I was out of options. If he'd gone off somewhere to sulk and had stepped outside the boundary, something might happen to him. When we went to Croagh Patrick, no one had followed or attempted to stop us, but it didn't mean we weren't being watched by whoever had taken his memories. Hannah had lured him away from the hawthorns, and look what happened.

Where are you? Come to me...

The low growling hummed behind me, and I turned, my eyes flying open.

A russet-colored fox was prowling around the clearing, his head down and his eyes flashing. *Boone!*

Darting across the clearing, I fell to my knees before him, ignoring his bared teeth.

"Boone!" I grabbed him by the scruff of the neck, my fingers digging into his waxy fur, and I shook him. "You're acting like a baby! Change back so I can talk to you!"

He yipped and growled, shaking himself and dislodging my grasp.

"Boone!" I said again, reaching for him. "Please!"

He danced around the clearing, clearly agitated. *Of all the stubborn foxes...*

"He tricked me," I said, tears forming in my eyes. "I went to tell him... I told him he would never win me back.

I…" *I love you.* The words stuck in my throat, and I raised my hand to my neck. "I…" *Why couldn't I say it?*

I wanted to scream it at the top of my lungs. I wanted to tell Boone he meant everything to me. He gave me his heart in this very spot, and I wanted to give him mine forever. *You hear that universe? Forever!*

"I…"

Boone stared at me, his fox eyes shining eerily in the half-light of twilight.

"I…" I tried to form the words, but I began to cough instead, choking on my declaration.

The fox growled and leaped away, disappearing into the darkening forest, leaving me all alone in the middle of the clearing.

Falling to my knees, I gasped for breath.

"I… L… *Lo*…"

Why couldn't I say it?

The next morning, I woke fully clothed, askew on the bed, one foot hanging off the edge and my arm flung over the other. I'd slept sideways on top of the quilt.

Lifting my head, I sniffed my armpit. I stunk like sheep shite. Somehow, I'd made it back to the cottage in one piece, but who knew how that eventuated.

Dragging myself out of bed and shuffling into the shower, I washed the filth off me, then slapped on some fresh clothes and a pound of makeup to disguise the bags under my eyes.

Outside, the day had hardly begun, and it was already dreary. The sun was hidden behind a thick layer of gray, dew was sticking to every available surface, and my breath was vaporizing on the air.

Screw winter.

Screw the snow.

Screw everything!

I had a score to settle.

I practically tore the village apart looking for Alex. I checked Mary's Teahouse, peered in the windows at Molly McCreedy's, walked through the car park, inquired at the bed-and-breakfast, but it was he who finally found me by St. Brigid's church.

"What are you doing lurking in a graveyard this time of morning?" he asked with a chuckle.

"You've gone too far," I said, turning on him. "There's a line, and you crossed it miles ago."

"*Whoa,*" he said, holding up his hands. "All I did was give you a little kiss."

"Get out of my life, Alex!"

"We both know that's not happening."

"Like hell, it isn't."

He grasped my arms and pulled me close, causing panic to spike. We were alone behind the church at the butt crack of dawn. Not even Father O'Donegal was pottering around inside preparing his sermon for Sunday. Something didn't feel right. The air tingled with an unknown energy, and I began to feel the same fear I'd experienced the night Boone and I had lured the craglorn to the hawthorn.

Lucy warned me, I thought. *She warned me about his malice...*

"Let go of me," I demanded, struggling against his grasp.

"Skye, don't fight me," he crooned. "You want to be

here. You want to be in my arms. You want to go back to Australia where things were easy. Don't you?"

I sank into his touch, his words making my head swim. Maybe he was right...

"You don't need these people," he went on. "You don't need Boone. He walked away from you, remember? You told him how you felt, and he didn't want you."

"I..." But I hadn't told him because the words had stuck in my throat.

"Shh," Alex murmured. "I'll make it all better. Just come with me, and you'll forget all about this place..."

He tugged at me once more, and I sank against him, pressing my cheek against his chest. His hand began stroking through my hair and over my shoulder, soothing the panic from my heart. Focusing on his fingers, I sighed. Maybe he was right.

I stilled as the air shimmered around us. It was so slight, I almost missed it, but for a second, his fingers had turned blue. Blue like the man I'd seen at Aileen's wake at Molly McCreedy's.

Remembering the image of the man who'd shimmered into a blue humanoid monster with long pointy teeth, and I gasped, breaking out of Alex's grip.

That was how they did it. *That was how they hid among us.*

I was almost too afraid to look Alex in the eye, but I raised my head, knowing if I was right, then I was in a shiteload of trouble.

The air shimmered, and his face was no longer the Alex I knew. His skin took on a sickly steely blue hue, his eyes bulged, his hair grew long and black, and his teeth became razor-sharp points. He appeared to me in his true form for the blink of an eye before his glamour returned.

Ew! He'd kissed me!

"No…" I murmured, taking a step back. "That was you… At Aileen's wake…"

He was a fae, and that kiss at the tower house had been a spell. He'd taken my ability to tell Boone I loved him. He'd stolen my words and destroyed Boone in the process.

He'd stolen my words!

At that moment, I should've been alarmed. In the least, I should've attempted to hold onto some kind of rational thought, but all I saw was the enemy. The enemy who'd taken Boone away from me. The enemy who'd divided us in order to get to me, the last Crescent.

The enemy.

Alex was a fae, and he was working with Carman…but was it Alex? Had they snatched his body and possessed him with magic? Or was he an illusion? Or, more worryingly, had he been a fae the whole time I'd known him? Before and after the Crescents called me home.

If I were thinking a little more clearly, then maybe I would've made a different choice. Maybe was a terrible word in hindsight. But my faculties were definitely not in order. They had been completely blown apart.

"You took my words!" I shrieked, seeing red. *"Give them back!"*

He chuckled and shook his head. "There's only one way you can do that."

I narrowed my eyes. He was talking to me like I should know, but I didn't. I didn't know how to break his stupid spell, and it was infuriating.

"You don't know how to use your magic," he stated, looking surprised. "That's new."

"You know shit all," I exclaimed. "You and that bitch Carman don't know anything about me."

Fae-Alex laughed, clearly not believing I was in control

of my Crescent abilities. I wasn't, and I didn't have the athame like I did when I fought the craglorn, but I knew how to smack him down. Magic was about instinct and intent…and boy, did I have a single intent when I looked at the fae who'd tricked us all.

He'd said there was only one way to break the spell he'd kissed on my lips. Death was the obvious choice and clearly, he thought I wasn't capable.

"Carman is coming for you," he said, laughing. "There's nothing you can do to stop her returning to Ireland. When she does, the doorways will be opened, and the witches will be punished. *You worst of all*. The Crescents will *suffer*."

"Do you know who you're talking to?" I demanded. "I am Skye Williams, *Crescent Witch*."

Raising my hand, I called on my magic and launched myself at him with a roar. His glamour dissolved as my power lashed out, revealing his true form.

We fell to the ground, and I straddled his body, not letting him go for a second. I felt the golden light stream from my hands and spear into his body, stabbing into his repulsiveness like I was wired with twin blades. I didn't need the athame this time because *I was the sword*.

"Skye," he said, moaning as my golden light engulfed him. "Skye, you're killing me…"

His face shifted back into the Alex I knew, but I didn't falter. Fae were tricksters. He was trying to pull on my heartstrings.

"Skye, please… *It hurts*…" He moaned and writhed, trying to knock me off him, but I was too strong.

Fae-Alex began to convulse, his eyes rolling into the back of his head. Then, he gasped and went rigid.

"*The spell will be broken*," he exclaimed in an

otherworldly voice. "*The blood of the golden one will crack the chains, and she will return…*"

"What are you talking about?" I shook him violently. "*Explain yourself!*"

Fae-Alex's eyes glazed over, and he went limp. My magic had run its course and taken what I'd willed it to.

"No!" I shook him again. "*No…*"

His body began to emit wafts of steam, and I scrambled off him with a yelp as he began to melt and dissolve. His face sagged and bubbled, and I covered my eyes.

He was dead. I'd killed him. *I'd killed Alex.*

Huddling against my mother's empty grave, I moaned, calling out for the one person I needed most but knew wouldn't come.

"*Boone!*"

CHAPTER 9

I ran all the way to Irish Moon.

By the time I got there, I was completely out of breath, and my lungs burned. Considering St. Brigid's was only a few hundred meters away, it was a sign I was terribly unfit.

Lucy was waiting for me out the front, a takeaway cup of coffee in her hands. When she saw me, her expression fell.

"Are you all right?" she asked. "You look terrible."

"Thanks," I said, making a face.

"Oh, I didn't mean… Has somethin' happened?"

"I'm really sorry, but I… I don't think I'm going to open the shop today. Something's come up, and it can't wait."

"Do you need any help?"

I shook my head, hoping no one had heard my argument and subsequent murder of Alex.

"I'll see you tomorrow?" I asked with a grimace.

"Tomorrow." She nodded enthusiastically. "If you need anything, you've got me phone number."

"Sure, thanks." As I caught my breath, I watched her walk across the road to where she usually parked her car behind Mary's Teahouse. "Hey, Lucy?"

She turned.

"Thanks," I said. "For understanding."

"Don't mention it." She smiled and continued on her way.

Shaking my head, I turned the corner and went around the back of the shop. That woman was super understanding. Mairead would've thrown an epic tantrum, then fleeced me for an extra fifty euros to look after the shop. I didn't like closing and losing a day's trade, but Boone was more important. He was the ultimate, you know?

I spent the day walking the forest right to the limits of the hawthorns, but Boone had disappeared. He had a strong animal nature, and if he didn't want to be found, then he wouldn't be found.

Completely defeated, I shuffled into Molly McCreedy's as the sun began to dip low, hoping someone would've seen or heard something.

Maggie was behind the bar, polishing a pint glass.

"Hey," I said, leaning against the bar. "Have you seen Boone?"

She gave me a dirty look and flicked her ringleted hair over her shoulder.

"*Maggie.*"

"Nay, no one's seen him for a few days," she said. "Not since… *You know.*"

"Give me a break."

"You broke his heart, flouncin' off with that Australian moron."

"I didn't flounce anywhere!" I exclaimed. "Have you seen him or not?"

"No, I haven't."

Turning, I surveyed the pub. A few groups of locals were sitting around tables by the fireplace, drinking and talking heatedly about something or other.

Listening closely, I heard Roy complaining about the absence of one of his farmhands.

"There's been a fox hangin' about the top fields," Roy said, sounding irritated. "Wherever that boy has vanished, I need him up there watchin' the flock."

"Get Sean up there with Phee," another man said.

"Nay," the old man replied. "I can't leave Sean alone for too long. I'm afraid he'll turn up drunk as a skunk and cut off a limb."

My heart sank. Boone hadn't shown up for work in two days, which wasn't like him at all. He was the guy who was always on time, always dependable, and always did his work to the highest standard. He even stayed late if he had to and refused to be paid overtime. To just vanish and not let anyone know was completely out of character.

I knew why he'd taken off, and it seemed like the entire village was currently debating which side they were going to take in the breakup. Team Skye, or Team Boone. Let's just say, it was shaping up like all my high school PE nightmares. You know, the ones where I was picked last and shoved in the back because I was the weakest link. I was totally the kid who forged notes from her parent so she could get out of all forms of team sports.

The group of men had realized I was staring at them while I was off daydreaming about my teenage years and were glaring at me.

Grimacing, I hightailed it across the room and shoved outside.

Boone was lurking around here someplace. All I had to do was be persistent. I would wander around the forest all night if I had to.

Burying into my jacket, I shoved my hands into my pockets and headed for the path behind Irish Moon. Luckily, I wasn't afraid of what lurked in the dark anymore. I'd conquered that fear weeks ago, but I hadn't faced the fear that even if I did find Boone, he mightn't want to come back at all.

Shoving away the terrible thought, I resumed my search. There was no other way.

The forest was dark, and the temperature was dropping.

Powering through the trees, I followed the paths, searching the night for the elusive fox. I reached the very edge of the boundary, then I turned back, looking in on the Druid's cave we'd once sheltered in during an unexpected rainstorm. The heavy scent of earth filled my nostrils, but it was empty inside.

The night wore on and I was really beginning to worry.

I doubted Boone had been in any animal form for more than a few hours. If I was right, then he'd been a fox for two days. The longer he was an animal, the harder it would be for him to change back. His wild instincts would take over, and he'd… No, it wouldn't come to that.

I carved a path through the forest, listening and searching for signs he'd been this way. I didn't know a single thing about tracking animals, but Boone wasn't an animal. Not yet, anyway.

The shrill cry of a fox broke through the air, and my head shot up. *Boone.*

I ran blindly toward the sound, desperate to catch him before he vanished. If he crossed the boundary and something happened to him, I would never forgive myself.

I'd been so stupid. I should've seen what Alex was hiding… *I should've known.*

My foot caught on an exposed root, and I fell. My shoulder hit the ground, jarring against the earth, and I rolled. Over and over I tumbled, careening down a slope until I crashed to a stop at the bottom, my back colliding with a fallen tree trunk.

"*Ow!*" I exclaimed, curling in on myself.

Gritting my teeth, I waited for the throbbing pain in my body to subside before moving. *Where was he?*

"Boone…" I moaned, pushing myself up. "Ow… Shite, that hurts…"

A low growl hummed on the still air, and I glanced up to find a fox sitting before me. He was watching me with a lowered head, his eyes flashing in the darkness.

"Boone?" I asked, knowing full well it was him. No fox would sit like that unless it scented the blood from all the grazes I'd gotten rolling down that hill and intended to eat me.

Impulsively, I reached out and sank my fingers into the fur either side of his face. He didn't run away or try to gnaw my hands off, so it was definitely him.

"Where have you been?" I asked. "Everyone's worried about you. They're already marking out territory for both of us."

He pulled back, tugging against my hold.

"Al—" I stopped myself abruptly. "You were right about him. *He was a fae.*" My grip loosened, and I sat back on my heels. "I… I took care of it, but I think you already felt my magic this morning, didn't you?"

Boone blinked but didn't move.

"So, there's irrefutable evidence that I'm stupid and need you more than ever."

He blinked again.

"I'm frightened," I went on. "Something's coming. Something really bad, and I don't know what to do."

I grasped his fur in my hands and pressed my nose against his snout.

"If you don't change back, I'm afraid you won't remember how. Boone, you've gotta come back. *Please*."

He growled and shook his head, breaking free. Taking a few steps back, he lowered his head and bared his teeth.

"I killed him," I declared, tears pricking in my eyes. "I killed Alex with my magic. He just…melted away, and that was it."

Some of the tension left Boone's body.

"I love you, Boone," I said with as much conviction as I could muster. "I've never loved anyone before you, do you hear me? It's you. *It'll always be you*."

He began to whimper, then let out a low keening sound. Shaking his head, I heard the snap of bones, and gradually, he began to change.

His snout shrank, his fur began to recede, and his legs started to grow into human arms and legs. His spine shuddered and snapped, and his tail merged into the small of his back. Before long, Boone was before me, crouched on all fours, his head bowed.

He trembled, giving away that his change had been more painful than usual. Not able to hold my tears any longer, I sobbed and threw my arms around his neck, forcing him to kneel.

"*Skye…*" he murmured, grasping my waist.

Pulling back, I traced my hands over his face, then his arms and chest, making sure he wasn't hurt…and verifying he was indeed real.

"Please, please, please," I muttered. "You can't leave me. I need you. It has nothing to do with magic or destiny or whatever. It's always been about you and me. *Boone…*"

"*Skye.*"

He sighed, then tilted my chin up. The moment our eyes met, something passed between us. Some kind of unspoken pledge entwined our destinies, and then he kissed me.

His lips were firm against mine, his touch desperate as I clung to him. I didn't care that he was completely naked or that we were kneeling in a ditch in the woods in the middle of the night.

When he finally pulled away, I whimpered in complaint, not willing to let him go.

"The wolf…" he began, clutching me tightly. "The first night I remember… I was runnin' from wolves in me fox form. I'd done somethin', but every time I try to remember, I can't. Me head splits open with a terrible pain. The wolf that attacked you… Who I was before… Carman… You used your magic again."

"Boone, slow down," I pleaded. "You're not making any sense."

"I think I brought it here. Me past brought it here, and whoever I was… It might kill you. Who I was might kill you."

"Brought what here? The craglorn was my fault… Alex… He was my fault, too. They're trying to trick us. They know we're nothing without each other."

"Nay…" he said. "Nay, the wolf."

"The…" Remembering the wolf that had attacked me right before I'd found out Boone was a shapeshifter, I tensed. "The wolf whose eye I poked out?"

"I think it was there for me. Me past. I…" He winced as the curse of his amnesia tore through his skull.

He was having trouble explaining his fears, but I understood without him putting all the words together. He was afraid whoever took his memories, and even what they contained, might come back and hurt me. That was why he was acting so weird. Alex showing up had just amplified everything.

My heart twisted, and I thrust my fingers through his hair. "Is that why you were so distant?"

"I… I didn't want to hurt you."

"I don't care who you were before," I said. "It doesn't matter. I know you *now*."

"Skye—"

"*Shh*," I said, placing a finger over his lips. "You don't have to worry about anything. They tried to break us apart. They tried, and they failed."

"You killed him…"

I tensed and dropped my gaze. "I had to. He was trying to lure me away." I swallowed hard. "I had to."

"He was a fae," he said as if he were trying to convince himself.

"He was a fae," I confirmed. "I saw his true face and felt his intent. He was going to take me from you. For Carman's epic revenge plot."

"No," he muttered. "She will never get her hands on you."

Boone grasped my face, and before I could catch my breath, he kissed me again, this time more feverish than the last. His tongue slid against mine, my temperature rising to unbearable. This was the moment he usually pulled away, but this time, there was nothing to keep us apart.

Laying me back in the soft leaf litter, he covered my body with his and continued his exploration. His lips traced the curve of my neck as his fingers unbuttoned my blouse, and the heat of his body fought off the chill of night.

"I love you, Skye," he murmured, his gaze meeting mine.

"I love you," I whispered before raising my head to catch him in a kiss.

CHAPTER 10

I never knew the throes of passion would lead me to this moment. This moment being sex in a ditch.

Nestling up against a very naked Boone, I clung to him for warmth. I never noticed how hot his body was. Literal temperature-wise, thank you. He emitted wave after wave of heat like he was a furnace.

"You're really warm," I said. "You're a big hot-water bottle."

"Must be me metabolism," he muttered. He picked up the talisman from where it lay between my breasts and began to study it. "You better get dressed. I don't want you catchin' a chill."

"With you keeping me warm? *Pfft.* I've finally got you naked."

"You've seen me naked lots of times," he said with a chuckle. "It's an occupational hazard."

"Not *naked* naked," I argued.

"Ahh," he said, his lips quirking. "The infamous cock sandwich."

I snorted and began giggling, but then a chill did

shudder through my body, and I sat up, looking for my shirt.

"Skye?"

"I, uh…" Finding my blouse, I pulled it on and began doing up the buttons.

Boone sat up, pressing his chest against my arm.

"What happened?"

"He found me by St. Brigid's," I replied. "I wanted to convince him to go home, but… It was like he was trying to cast a spell on me. When you saw him kiss me, that's what he did. I tried to tell you how I felt the other night, but he took my words. Boone, I didn't…"

"*Shh*," he murmured, untangling my hair with his fingers. "I know it now at least."

"I'm sorry. I didn't mean for it to get this far."

His brow creased, and he pressed his forehead against my shoulder, hiding his face from me.

"Boone?"

"Aye, don't worry yourself about it," he murmured, meeting my gaze. "It hurt knowin' I might lose you. It was worse thinkin' you didn't love me."

"But I never—"

"Skye." His hand turned around my knee, sending warmth through my skin. "I believe you."

"I need you so much," I whispered, resting my forehead against his.

He cupped my cheek and then kissed me softly on the lips. His touch was slow and tender, his stubble scratching my skin, and I sank into him with a sigh. Man, he was *good*.

Licking my lips, I found my underwear and shimmied into them before adding my jeans to the mix.

"Do all fae look like that?" I asked.

"Like what?"

"Like bluish-gray monsters with pointed teeth."

Boone frowned and shook his head. "No. No, they don't."

"It was like he had a spell cast over him to make him look human. A glamour." I glanced at him warily. "Do you think he was always like that? Was he always a fae?"

"I don't know."

I saw the look on his face. It mirrored what I felt inside my heart. If Alex had always been a fae, then he'd never wanted me. All that time we'd spent together as a couple had been a lie. And if it were true, then I'd just killed the same man I'd shared my life with.

"He delivered a prophecy," I murmured. "Right before he died, his eyes went all misty, and he spoke in a strange voice. That's prophesying, right?"

"What did he say?"

"*The spell will be broken. The blood of the golden one will crack the chains, and she will return…*"

"It does sound strange."

"They need my blood to break the spell that's keeping her out of Ireland," I said. "If he's right…"

"I don't believe in prophecy," Boone said.

"If he's right, then there's nothing we can do. They might already have what they need…"

"Skye, prophecies aren't always straightforward. It may not be so cut-and-dry."

"Sounds pretty straightforward to me. I'm the golden one because my magic is golden. My blood will break the curse my coven put on Carman to stop her from returning. Can't get any more cut-and-dried as that."

Boone tensed, and I glared at him.

"What?"

"Skye…" He stroked his hand through my hair.

"I used my magic," I said, tugging on my socks. "We need to keep watch."

"Aye," Boone murmured. "Don't worry. If somethin' comes, we know what we're doin' this time."

I sighed, hoping I'd flown under the radar. It was a fool's hope because Alex had been an agent of Carman. When he didn't show up to report, she would know something had happened to him. That something being death by Crescent.

"We'll figure it out," he said, handing me a boot. "We've done all right so far."

"So far." I zipped the side of one boot closed and shoved my foot into the other.

Boone rose to his feet, then held out his hands for me. Taking them in my own, he hauled me upright and immediately embraced me. A naked Irishman and a disheveled witch. What a sight we had to be.

"Meet me back at the cottage?" I asked.

"Aye," he replied. "One tabby cat comin' right up."

I turned my back as he changed, and once he was done, he rubbed against my leg.

Scooping him up into my arms, I carried him back toward Derrydun, my heart a little lighter.

When I woke the next morning, I found a handsome Irishman in bed next to me.

Rolling over, I studied Boone's face, memorizing his features. I'd never realized how long his eyelashes were before. They brushed against his cheeks, adding to his boyish charm. He needed to shave badly, his stubble was out of control, but he always did. Maybe the fast beard growth was to do with his shapeshifter metabolism…just like his six-pack was because I never saw him go to the gym. Mainly because there wasn't one anywhere near Derrydun.

Realizing I was watching him sleep, I sat up and fumbled for my phone. I was totally being a creep.

Despite everything that had happened with Boone and me last night, Alex was still on my mind. Opening up my social media app—that I'd hardly even looked at since arriving in Ireland—I scrolled through my paltry friends list and found his profile. Tapping on his name, my eyes widened as I saw he'd marked himself in a relationship and tagged a woman who I'd never heard of before. Being a total stalker, I opened her profile and checked her out. She was blonde, skinny, tanned, and the total opposite of me. Even her teeth were perfect.

He'd gone from being single to in a relationship in the space of five months, but so had I. That little pang I felt? Totally an overreaction considering I killed his potential body double yesterday.

Sighing, I went back to Alex's timeline and checked out his most recent posts. His last one was time stamped during the night, alleviating some of the guilt I felt at choking fae-Alex to death with Crescent magic. I would have to call him, but it looked to me the real Alex was alive and well back in Australia where I'd left him…all moved on and shacking up with another woman. Glancing at Boone, I smirked.

"What're you smilin' at?" he asked sleepily.

"Your eyes are closed," I declared. "How do you know I'm even looking at you, huh?"

"Then it was an amazin' guess."

Flopping back down in bed, I snuggled against him, still holding my phone.

"What's that?" he asked, kissing my shoulder and wrapping his arm around my waist.

"A phone."

"Very funny."

"I just… I wanted to look up Alex and make sure he…" I felt my cheeks reddening, and I turned my face away.

"You wanted to make sure he was still alive?"

"Yeah." I lifted my phone and stared at the screen. "It wasn't really him. That thing…it must've taken his face and memories."

Boone's eyes narrowed, and I rolled mine.

"He's not coming here anytime soon," I declared. "He's moved on, and so have I."

"Good."

"We had sex in a ditch, you do realize that?"

Boone laughed and held me tighter.

"I don't get naked in the middle of nature for just anyone." I pouted.

"Then I feel blessed."

"What are we going to tell everyone?"

"About the ditch?" He raised an eyebrow. "Nothin'."

"*No*, about us." I pinched him on the ass. "I went into Molly McCreedy's last night looking for you, and everyone was discussing territory."

"Territory?" he asked. "What does that mean?"

"Like Irish Moon is Skye territory. Molly McCreedy's is neutral. Roy's farm is Boone territory."

"Really?"

"Yes, really. Roy's also got a bee in his bonnet about a

fox that's been hanging around the sheep. Know anything about that?"

"I'm dedicated to me work," he said with a pout.

"I figured it was you." I made a face. "You didn't get hungry for lamb chops?"

"Nay. It didn't get that far."

"I hope not because that's kinda gross."

He chuckled and leaned over me to check the time on the alarm clock. "Speakin' of Roy, I better get up. I've got some patchin' up to do."

"Sure."

He kissed me on the lips, his hand tightening on my waist.

"I'll see you later?"

"Ditch or cottage, your pick," I quipped.

"Very funny."

Listening to him potter about in the bathroom, I smiled. This was how I pictured things after our battle with the craglorn. The easy conversation, the 'I love yous,' and the sex. *Oh, the sex...* My toes curled, and I stretched, remembering the punch line.

I didn't even care that I had a bruise on my ass from rolling down that hill in the dark.

Well, maybe I cared a little when I sat down...

When I finally dragged myself around the corner to Irish Moon, Lucy was waiting for me.

"Hey," she said. "Did you get everythin' sorted yesterday?"

"Yeah," I said, fishing the keys out of my pocket. "The mini crisis was averted."

Unlocking the door, I let us inside. The air felt different in here today. Usually, Irish Moon was full of a warm energy that had everything to do with the abundance of crystals packed into every nook and cranny, but in the last week, things had been slightly off-kilter. That morning, things seemed to be back to normal, so I gathered it must've had something to do with Fae-Alex and his funny business. Whatever magical trickery seeds he'd been sewing must've died the moment he carked it.

Okay, saying he 'carked it' was a little insensitive, but since he turned out to be a fae with a penchant for identity theft, then maybe it wasn't as callous as it sounded.

I watched Lucy cross the shop floor and disappear out the back. A moment later, the lights flicked on, and she reappeared, taking the initiative to get to work on her own.

Thinking about how I'd seen her arguing with Fae-Alex the other day, I narrowed my eyes. She must've said something gnarly because he'd seemed nervous around her. Why?

"What did you say to Alex?" I asked. "The other day when I saw you talking to him outside. What did you say?"

"Nothin'," she replied with a shrug. "I just told him to get a clue. I could see he was botherin' you, and I mean… How many times can a woman say no before a man gets it? If I overstepped, I'm sorry…"

Sighing, I waved my hand. "It's all right."

"Was that what happened yesterday?" she asked sheepishly.

I couldn't really tell her the sordid truth, so I just nodded and offered a watered-down version. "We had a long talk, and he accepted my feelings had changed. He left Derrydun yesterday."

"Oh, that's good, then. Are things okay with you and your boyfriend?"

"Boone and I had a long talk, too." I shrugged, smiling at the thought of our romp through nature. "We're solid."

Lucy smiled and began straightening the stand of wind chimes. "Good for you."

Rounding the counter, I searched for my tarot cards. Yeah, it was good for me. Boone and I were back to a good place, he'd voiced his fears, and I had mine, and now we could work through them. All while protecting the village from the threat of craglorn attacks. Then there was the prophecy to worry about.

I rolled my eyes and began shuffling the cards.

"Hey, Lucy?" I asked. "Do you believe in prophecies?" If anyone knew about the truth of these things, maybe it was her. She was the Irish version of *Lara Croft, Tomb Raider* with her archaeology and mythological studies skills.

"Prophecies?" She raised her eyebrows, then scrunched up her face in thought. "I don't think I do. They're kind of like your tarot cards, I suppose."

"Like a suggestion?" I considered that idea and shook my head. "Have any ever come true? I mean, in history?"

"They feature in myths and legends in lots of cultures," she went on. "But none have been proven. Not for certain, anyway. The problem is, words can be twisted to the point people see and hear what they want to believe. There was a story in the news a while ago about a blind old woman in Romania who supposedly predicted nine eleven in America and other disasters, though it was after the fact when it came out in the mainstream media. All her predictions since haven't born any fruit, or so the sayin' goes. Honestly, it's hard to say. There has to be an element of belief."

"So you have to believe in a prophecy to give it any merit?"

"Who knows." She laughed and shrugged. "What brought this on?"

"Oh, nothing," I said, turning back to the tarot cards. "Just a little early morning existential crisis."

Shuffling the deck, I pulled a card from the middle and set it down on the counter. *Please, not the Three of Swords, please, not the Three of Swords…*

Turning the card over, I swore.

CHAPTER 11

"Are you ready?"

"Do we have to?" I glanced at Boone and screwed up my nose.

"Aye, we'll have to show our faces eventually." He nodded at Molly McCreedy's, which we were standing outside of. "Once they see us together again, the battle lines will be erased, and things will go back to the way they were."

"I'm not sure that's any better." I looked at Fergus's donkey, which was hitched to a post with her nose in a feed bag. "What do you think?"

Boone placed his palm on her rump and smirked. "She thinks her oats are really good."

I snorted and rolled my eyes. "A true Irish donkey."

He grasped my hand and tugged me forward. Opening the door, he had to practically drag me inside. I knew how things worked around here. First in first out and all of that. Right after Aileen's funeral, Boone had told me I'd always be welcome here. I was part of the McKinney clan—McKinney was Aileen's maiden name—and apparently, it was like some kind of birthright. I doubted it meant much around here after Boone and my public fight over Alex even if I was magically linked to the land.

I squirmed as I felt a dozen or more pairs of eyes focus on us. Waiting for the various opinions to begin hurling through the air, I tensed, ready to deflect the word bullets.

"Did she cast a spell on you?" Sean called out across the bar.

"Shut it, Sean," I exclaimed.

"Leave him to me," Boone said, dropping my hand and going to sit by the farmer.

I watched as he patted Sean on the shoulder and began talking earnestly to him. Glancing around the pub, I scurried toward the bar, looking for Maggie.

She was behind the taps, pulling a pint of beer, and she raised an eyebrow as I slid onto a stool.

"You and Boone are back on?" she asked, nodding toward the men at the other end of the mahogany slab.

"Yeah. It was a big misunderstanding."

"What happened to that Australian twat?" She gave me the evil eye.

"He twatted back to where he came from," I said irritably. "Don't be angry with me. He was the one who caused the trouble. Boone knows it, I know it. We're good. Are you and I? Because it wasn't really anyone's business other than ours."

"I told you, Skye, Derrydun looks out for its own."

"And what am I? Haven't I earned enough stripes or whatever yet?"

"None of it was Skye's fault," Boone said, sidling up next to me.

"You believe her?" Sean grumbled.

Boone glanced at me. "She said no, and he kept

pressurin' her. I kept showin' up at the wrong moments. He was a crafty *mac soith*."

"I hope you gave him another thrashin'," Maggie quipped.

"What's the score on the scoreboard," I declared. "Do I register yet?"

"Calm down, Skye," Maggie said. "You're a *Derrydunerian*."

"Good." I pouted.

The noise in the pub began to creep back up, and the ears of the rumor mill turned to other juicy topics.

"See?" Boone said. "I told you it would be all right."

"I still think she's a witch," Sean declared, earning him a sharp clip around the ear from Maggie. "*Ow!*"

"What's your problem, Sean McKinnon!" she screeched.

"Should I worry about that?" I asked Boone.

"Nay. He's just stirrin' the pot because he knows you bite."

"Good, I was worried I might have to turn him into a toad to teach him a lesson."

He laughed and gave me a kiss on the cheek. "I see Mark Ashlyn over there. I just want to have a word, and then I'll be back. Think you can hold onto your magic until then?"

"It'll be a struggle, but I think I'll manage." I made a face and waved him off.

The moment I was free, I sensed someone creeping up in my blind spot. Turning, I saw it was Roy.

"Skye," he said, sitting beside me. "Mary wants to know if you like lavender."

"Lavender?" I made a face. Why was Roy asking me about smelly flowers?

"They flower in summer she says. Her reasonin' is you and Boone will have a bit more time together to solidify your relationship. Spring is too soon. Her words, not mine."

My mouth fell open. They were still planning our supposed wedding!

"So?" he asked. "Do you like lavender?"

After the standoff in Molly McCreedy's, things seemed to get back to normal. At least, as normal as things usually were in Derrydun.

Autumn was in full swing. Leaves were changing color, rain was falling more often than not, the fog was rolling in most mornings, and among all of it, Boone had practically moved into the cottage. He kept me warm in bed and cooked me breakfast every morning.

Lucy was doing well at Irish Moon, but I wasn't ready to give her the reins solo yet. She wasn't Mairead, but she was fun to hang around, which made the workday go a hell of a lot faster. Speaking of the Goth girl, I hadn't heard from her since she went off to Trinity College. I took it as a good sign and hoped the talisman I'd given her had protected her delicate parts from STDs.

We'd also been on the lookout for any wayward craglorns and other assorted magical tricksters that might've sensed the magical flare I'd sent up when I'd attacked Fae-Alex, but nothing had stirred. It seemed we'd gotten lucky, but it was a notion I wasn't too keen to rely on.

I considered Derrydun to be at DEFCON three. Ready for decisive action at the slightest provocation.

We were at Molly McCreedy's enjoying the latest addition to the menu, a side of colcannon with our lamb chops.

"Have you had it before?" Boone asked, watching me poke my fork at it.

"No."

"It's just potato, cabbage, and kale."

"Cabbage?" I pinched my nose. "You can't stay over tonight unless your farts smell like roses."

He laughed and shoveled some into his mouth like a pig.

"I'm serious, you know."

"People used to leave out bowls of colcannon for the fairies and goblins," he said once he'd swallowed.

"If you'd told me that me a couple of months ago, I would've laughed at you," I said. "But now, I totally believe it."

"They used to put trinkets inside for people to find, too."

"Like what?"

"Coins, mostly. Sometimes rings and other things, but that was a long time ago." He waved his fork. "Whatever you found would be like a lucky charm for the year to come. A coin for wealth, a ring for marriage, and so on."

"Oh, like a plum pudding at Christmas," I exclaimed. "When I was little, and my grandma was still with us, she used to bake five-cent pieces in them. Well, until Dad almost choked on one. And now that I think of it, that sounds kind of gross. Can you get poisoned from cooking coins into pudding?"

Boone laughed and shrugged. "You're still alive, so I guess not."

"Does Derrydun have a big Christmas?" I asked,

thinking about the holiday. It was the first week of September, which meant it was about three months until the big day.

"Last year, there was a dinner here at the pub," Boone replied. "Aileen cooked up a storm."

"Did she?"

Thinking about my mother, I frowned. I'd recently come to terms with her leaving me as a child, after all the Crescent Witch calling nonsense, but never knowing her really bothered me sometimes. Then there was Boone and the relationship he'd had with her. He'd lived at the cottage for something like three years before I came along. Now he lived somewhere outside of the village in some shack or tent or something.

"Boone?"

"Yeah?"

"Why haven't I seen your place yet?"

He set down his plate that I was certain he was about to lick and shrugged.

"If you want to come over, then you can come over," he said nonchalantly. "It's not as nice as your cottage, though."

"I'd still like to see it."

"Then, let's go see it." He smiled.

Relieved there was no big secret, I waited while he returned our dirty plates to the kitchen. Donning my coat, I went outside and patted Fergus's donkey, scratching her ears until Boone appeared.

We walked through the night hand in hand, our silence easy as we approached Boone's little cottage. It was a one-story whitewashed number with a modern tiled roof with an awkward television aerial stuck on top. There were a few pots out the front where he was growing some herbs and a couple of flowers, though the rest of the garden was grass. The whole scene was bordered by a stone drywall just like the one that surrounded the fields up on the hill.

Boone unlocked the door and let me inside, turning on the lights as I went. Immediately, I was hit with a smell that was strange yet oddly alluring. In a completely weird and sick way because it stunk.

"What's that smell?" I asked, curling up my nose.

"What smell?"

"You've got a super animal nose, and you can't smell that?"

"I assume you're talkin' about me natural musk," he said with a chuckle. "I can't smell me own smell."

"Is that what you call it?" I made a face and stepped further inside. "Natural musk?"

"Boone Number Five?" he quipped, making a joke.

"More like Ode de Boy Stink."

The cottage was definitely a man cave. His love for black and red check shirts had translated to his decor choice. A brown leather couch sat in front of an open fireplace, a small flat-screen television was jammed up against the wall to the side, a matching coffee table was littered with old books, papers, and several dirty coffee cups. On the other side of the hall, I caught sight of the kitchen, which was fairly clean and sparse considering he was such a great cook. I wondered if Aileen had taught him or if it was one of those ingrained skills that had followed him from his past.

There were two more rooms I could see at the back of the little cottage, which I assumed were his bedroom and a bathroom. It was tiny, and there wasn't much to see, but it seemed to suit Boone perfectly.

He led me into the little living room, and I sat on the

couch, shucking off my leather jacket. I watched as he lit the fire, throwing on some kindling and blowing on the little flame until it caught. Then he added some logs, arranging them in a carefully considered pile. I couldn't light a fire to save myself, so I would never be an arsonist, though I wondered if I could get around my lack of skill with magic.

At the thought of magic, my train of thought lost their brakes and went on a joyride across the network.

"Are you worried about somethin'?" Boone asked, sitting beside me on the couch. "You've got that look on your face."

"A lot of things worry me," I said. "Hang on. What look?"

"You screw up your nose, and you get that furrow between your brows." He placed his finger between my eyes.

"Do not."

He smiled. "Tell me about it."

Where did I begin?

"Can I light a fire with my magic?" I began, spitting out whatever came to mind. "Where are the other witches? We're so alone out here with no way to connect to the outside world. I'm meant to save people I've never met. The enemy is all around, and we can't see them until they show up on the front porch. They can sure as hell see us, so why can't we go and find them? We should be able to go on the offensive, too. I'm not good at waiting. I don't like it."

"That's a lot of things to worry about."

I shrugged.

"Boone?"

"Hmm?"

"We haven't really talked about what you told me…"

"About?"

"Your past…"

"Ah." He pulled me into his lap.

Nestling against his chest, I ran my fingertips along his jaw, delighting in the scratch of his stubble.

"I try not to dwell on it too much," he went on. "Whoever took me memories must have done a very good job. I try to avoid the headaches."

"The wolf that attacked me, you thought he was there for you?"

"Aye," he whispered. "It was wolves who were chasin' me. It's been years since that night… I thought they may have been becomin' impatient."

"You never crossed the boundary in all that time?"

"Only twice," he said, furrowing his brow.

I knew one of the times had been with me when we went to Croagh Patrick to charge the athame. The other had been when Aileen died protecting him from Hannah, the spriggan. At the thought of my mother, my heart felt heavy.

"Was there a reason you were worried?" I murmured. "I mean, to be with me?"

"I…" He swallowed hard, and I watched his Adam's apple bob up and down. "I worry sometimes. About who I was before."

"Me too," I admitted.

"You have?"

"And I told you it doesn't matter. Not to me." I placed my hand on his chest and felt his heartbeat, using a tiny trickle of magic to sense the thrum out. "You want to know what I think?"

"Desperately."

I smiled and continued, "They say people never change, at least, not at their core. So whoever you were before, if you were good or bad, you both shared the same heart. You must've been loyal, fierce, strong, and a total smart cookie."

"Trust you to make this about food."

"I do like cookies." I laughed and nuzzled closer, jamming my forehead against his neck.

"Skye… There's somethin' I never told you about that night."

"What night?"

"The night Hannah lured me outside the boundary."

I tensed and pulled away slightly. "There's something worse than being lured by the higher fae that killed Aileen?"

He lowered his gaze, and his teeth tugged on his bottom lip.

"*Boone.*"

"She told me somethin'…"

"About?" I was starting to lose my temper. Trying to get Boone to admit to something was like trying to get blood out of a stone.

"Hannah…" He almost clammed up again but went on. "I've had a lot of time to think about that night. When she revealed her true self to me, I recognized her form, though I hadn't seen anythin' like her before that night. She seemed to know me. Then…"

"Then?"

"She said Carman wanted me."

I froze, a million and one scenarios exploding in my mind, none of which I wanted to acknowledge.

"Skye… What if I was one of them?"

He'd told me Hannah wanted to give him to Carman

before, so it wasn't news, but to think she wanted him because he was in league with her? I couldn't believe it.

"It could mean anything," I argued. "It doesn't mean you were…" I couldn't even say it. "You could've attacked her, or you could've been a spy, or—"

"Skye," he said, interrupting me. "It's nice of you to think so, but there's no way to know."

"What if we found a way to unlock your memories? Then you would."

"Aileen already tried," he said somberly.

"And what did she say?"

"That me mind had been locked by a powerful spell, and the only way it could be undone was by the person who had the key." He glanced at me, the worry clear in his eyes. He thought Carman was the witch who took his memory.

"Are you happy?" I asked. "With who you are now? Are you happy?"

He frowned. "I have to be."

"You don't have to do anything," I countered. "If it bothers you that much, we can go find whoever messed with your past."

"Skye…"

"If it's her, then two birds with one stone." I shrugged, knowing what I was proposing was foolish, but if it helped Boone, then I would do it.

"Nay, I'm happy," he said. "It bothers me sometimes, but I'm safe here in Derrydun, and I have you. If unlockin' me memories means forcin' you to face your destiny before you're ready, then I don't want to know."

"You can't tell me you never think about who your parents might be?" I murmured. "Or what your name was? Or if you left anyone behind?"

Boone stared at me, then winced as a headache tore through his temples. Raising my hands, I pressed my thumbs against his forehead and began rubbing slow circles, coaxing my magic to soothe the sting of his attempt at reconciling his memories.

"I do think about it," he whispered as the pain eased. "I had this whole other life I'm disconnected from. But it's gone, Skye. Who that man was, I don't know him. He's a stranger."

Oh, Boone… He'd been distant because he'd believed Carman might use him to get to me. Wolves had been chasing him the first night he arrived in Derrydun just like the wolf that appeared at the hawthorn and attacked me. Thanks to Hannah, he'd thought he was to blame for it almost eating me. I also suspected he believed everything that had happened since his arrival was his fault.

They weren't in the slightest.

"Promise me," I said, grasping his face in my hands. "Promise me properly this time."

"Anythin'."

"Promise me you'll never keep any secrets, and I'll do the same. If something is bothering you, talk to me about it. Me, too. I don't want to go through another breakup. I wouldn't survive it."

"I promise." His hand grasped my thigh, and he squeezed. "I more than promise. It's me vow."

"Our greatest strength is our bond," I said, sounding all philosophical. "If we have that, then they can't hurt us. Screw their prophecy."

"One day at a time." He leaned in for a kiss.

"Sounds good to me."

CHAPTER 12

The following morning, I moseyed on into Irish Moon feeling happier than I had in a while.

The witchy life was never going to be easy breezy, but at least Boone and I were in a good place. And now that I'd seen his place and dispelled the mystery over his sleeping arrangements, we could go back to staying at mine. It didn't reek of boy at the cottage.

We parted ways in the garden that morning with a risqué kiss. Then he went off to Roy's to work the fields, and I skipped around to Irish Moon. We were the perfect couple, *finally*.

I also ignored the tarot cards and didn't bother drawing another. Nothing could burst my bubble today. *Nothing.* At least until twelve o'clock rolled around, and my stomach began to growl, demanding to be fed like a pouty toddler.

"I'm just going to get some lunch before the next bus rolls in," I said to Lucy, who was pottering around the shop, straightening the stock after the last stampede. "You'll be right for a sec?"

"Sure."

"Can I get you anything?"

She shook her head. "I brought me own lunch today, but thanks."

It was freezing outside, so I darted across to Mary's Teahouse as quickly as my feet would carry me. Pushing into the neon pink cottage, I was hit square in the face with a wall of blissful heat.

"Hi, Mary," I called out as I closed the door behind me.

The older lady shuffled out of the kitchen and smiled when she saw me beside the counter.

"Skye," she exclaimed. "Are you back for lunch again?"

"I can't get enough of your chicken and salad sandwiches. You know that." Eyeing off the display of cookies on the counter, I pointed to the double chocolate chip. "Throw in one of those for dessert if you wouldn't mind."

She clucked her tongue and reached for the sandwich she'd already prepared, knowing I was coming in all along. Man, I loved Mary. When it came to food and divining the future of it, she was pure magic.

She slid it into a white paper bag, then added the cookie.

"You know what?" I said. "Put in an extra cookie for Lucy."

"How is she gettin' along?" Mary asked, slipping another treat into the paper bag with my sandwich.

"She's great. She's great with the customers and actually interested in working, you know?"

"That's fantastic. Good for you."

"She's no Mairead, but she's pretty close."

Mary made a face, and I chuckled. It wasn't any secret

she didn't understand the Goth girl and her fashion choices, but at least it was innocent. Mairead had told me stories about being bullied at school because of her black lipstick.

"Tell me, Skye," she began, looking shifty. "What do you think of chicken and lamb for the mains?"

"What?"

"I know you kids like to have a vegetarian option, but I'm still workin' on some recipes."

"Options for what?"

"We need to lock in these things early. There's a lot of plannin' for a weddin' of this size. We can't just slap a few sandwiches on a plate and call it a day." She clucked her tongue.

"Mary!" I exclaimed. "Boone and I are not getting married!"

"You say that now…" She waggled her finger at me. "But when you find a good man, you better get a ring on your finger quick smart. There are plenty of sharks out there waitin' to take a bite, Skye."

I let out a frustrated cry and snatched up my sandwich. Storming across the teahouse, I shoved the door open with a violent jab.

"Remember the sharks, dear!" Mary called out after me. "And let me know what Boone thinks about the menu!"

What was with this village and their obsession with marrying me off to Boone? I loved him, but we'd only been together like two months or however long it had been. I hadn't exactly marked it on my calendar. I wasn't into shotgun weddings. Besides, there was nothing to shotgun. My uterus had never been occupied, past or present, thank you very much!

Stomping across the street, I opened the door to Irish Moon and stopped dead in my tracks.

Lucy was mucking around with the tumbled stones, forcing them up into the air. She was making them float, her fingers twisting and turning, manipulating their trajectory. *Lucy was a witch!* I could sense her magic as clear as day.

I let out a dramatic gasp, and my grip loosened on my sandwich and cookies. They fell to the floor with a *plop*, and Lucy turned around, her mouth falling open.

"It's not what it looks like," she declared, the stones falling back into the display.

"*Noooooo*," I said, drawing out the word. "I knew you were too good to be true!"

"Am not!"

"Are too!" I pointed my finger at her. "You're a witch!"

"So are you!"

"I can't believe I bought you a cookie!"

"You bought me a cookie?"

I chased her around the display, firing off questions.

"Why didn't you tell me?" I asked. "If you knew, then why didn't you say?"

"You know what it's like," she said, backing away. "You know what's out there."

"But we're on the same side!"

"Really? I've known others who would sell out their own children for a bit of favor."

"Seriously? That's terrible!"

"Power corrupts," she said defiantly.

She had a point.

"Why are you working here?" I asked, narrowing my eyes. "What do you want from me? Are you a spy?"

"No!" she declared. "I'm not!"

"Are you sure? Because I'm pretty sure you knew or at least suspected what Alex was."

She paled and ceased her fleeing.

"If you suspected, then why didn't you warn me?" I demanded. "He almost dragged me away!"

"You're one of them," she said with a squeak.

"One of them?" I exclaimed. "What's that supposed to mean?"

"Don't tell me you don't know your own family history. You're a Crescent Witch!"

Her tone of voice made it sound like she was calling me a Crescent bitch. Like I was some self-important, stuck-up princess with her head in the clouds. Boone had referred to the Crescents as the most powerful coven in Ireland before their decline in the wake of Carman's betrayal, but I didn't know anything about that. I might be the last member, but I wasn't a name.

"Four months," I said. "Four months and…" I counted the days on my fingers. "Two weeks. That's how long I've known. I never knew my mother, I never knew the coven, and I sure as hell don't know you!"

She cringed, clearly frightened of me.

"How did you know who I was, but I couldn't tell who you were?" I demanded, almost stomping on my sandwich.

"Everyone thought the Crescents were over," she said. "I didn't believe them!"

"Who? Where are the other witches? Why won't they show themselves?"

"You know why," Lucy exclaimed. "They're afraid of losing their magic!"

"So I'm left to fight on my own?" I demanded. "How is that fair?"

"You're a Crescent," she said again like it was the answer to everything.

"So?" I threw my hands up into the air. "It's not an excuse to hide like cowards! Do you really think I can protect an entire country on my own? Huh?"

"Skye, I didn't…"

"Didn't what?" I placed my hands on my hips and waited.

"When we heard about the last Crescent passin', we thought that was it. We might be able to come out of hidin'."

I stared at her, my expression falling. "What does that mean? You don't want me?"

"I know you don't mean it," Lucy said, stumbling over her words. "You can't help bein' born."

The prophecy. My blood was the key to breaking the chains—the chains being the curse that barred Carman from Ireland. Since my ancestors had locked the fae realm, I was the sole key to opening the doorways. She'd been collecting magic for a thousand years, and all she needed was a way to get close to the hawthorns, which was where the prophecy came into play.

The Crescents were at the heart of this whole war, and I was to blame for everyone's pain and suffering by simply being born. Now I knew why I'd never met any witches. They hated my guts because of the color of my magic.

"No, I don't mean it," I said sharply. "I never asked for any of this. I never asked to be the sole soldier in a war for a people I've never met, and now you're telling me they don't even want me? I didn't start this war, but I've been lumped with it all the same."

I picked up my sandwich from the floor and peered

inside the bag. It was still good, and so were the cookies. *My cookies.*

"Skye—"

"You can go home for today," I interrupted, not wanting to hear it. "Maybe I'll be more amicable about being an epic pain in the ass to the people I'm supposed to protect, no questions asked, tomorrow."

Turning my back, I took out my sandwich and began unwrapping it. Behind me, the bell above the door jingled, signaling Lucy had fled. Only time would tell if she came back.

Here I was all ready to go into battle against an unknown power that might kill me, and my own people would rather I die than even try to defeat the biggest evil of all?

Shoving a cookie into my mouth, I sighed, spitting crumbs across the counter.

What an epic slap in the face.

"I knew she wasn't all that!" I declared as I stormed across the top field, barely missing a pile of sheep droppings.

Boone raised his head and proceeded to look perplexed.

"What are you talkin' about?" he asked as the sheep scattered.

Phee streaked across the side of the hill after them, herding the black and white puffballs back into a neat pack.

"Lucy!" I declared, putting my hands only hips. "I caught her!"

He straightened up and dusted off his hands on his

jeans. "Caught her doin' what? Was she stealin' out of the till or somethin'?"

"No! She was making the tumbled stones float! She's a witch!"

Boone's mouth formed an *O* shape.

"So we were both right, thank you very much."

"You thought she was a fae," he countered.

"Don't make this into an argument."

"You're the one who stormed up here," he said, trying not to laugh.

"Why aren't you outraged?"

"If she's a witch, then I would hope she's on our side?" he offered.

"I can't believe it," I said, seething. "She hid from us this whole time."

"You can't blame her for that. We live in troubled times. It's been this way our whole lives when you think of it. For centuries even. Growin' up and havin' to keep what you are a secret? That would have to sew some seeds of mutual distrust, don't you think?"

My shoulders sank, and I rolled my eyes. "Why do you have to be so wise?"

"Someone has to be calm and level headed."

I slapped him on the arm, and he laughed, moving out of range.

"What happened? Did she say why she hid what she is?" he asked once I'd calmed down.

I shrugged. "I'm more worried why she took a job at Irish Moon in the first place."

"Why did she?"

"Stuffed if I know. She spoke about me like I'm the messiah who has to do this all on my own or else!" I felt like stomping my foot on the ground. "Where does it say I have to fight Carman solo in the witchy handbook? Robert O'Keeffe—wherever he's slunk off to—never mentioned there was fine print when he zapped me with that golden pen of his!"

"He's a leprechaun—*I think*—so he's only concerned with things that directly affect him."

"Typical male."

Boone laughed and tucked a loose strand of hair behind my ear. This Lucy thing was rather alarming, and his reaction hadn't soothed me at all. He was so calm and collected about life-threatening events it drove me up the wall. He was the same when the craglorn came looking for a snack.

"She said the witches are pissed that the Crescents didn't die out with Aileen. Why would they say that?" I felt a wave of tears welling in my eyes. "It's the prophecy. My blood can bring Carman back to Ireland."

"But it can also stop her. Don't forget that. It sounds like Lucy's fear is talkin'."

"I don't trust her."

"Then don't trust her," Boone shot back. "But don't make her out to be a villain until you know for sure. Fear can do strange things to people."

"I didn't tell her about you."

"Good, I suppose. But if she's a witch, then she might already sense somethin' off about me."

"Really? Is that why I can feel your aura?" I lifted my hands into the air and felt the space around him. If anyone were watching us, they would be scratching their head right about now. "That's not a sexual magnetism thing?"

"Nay," he said with a chuckle. "More like animal magnetism."

Phee barked, starting to get bored waiting for us, and sat at Boone's feet.

"Play it safe," he went on, scratching the border collie behind the ears. "Figure her out, but don't get too close. She might be able to help you with your magic. You've been complainin' about not knowin' any other witches."

"I'm still outraged." I pouted.

"You wouldn't be Skye if you weren't."

"What's that supposed to mean?"

"It means, I have to make a break for it before you realize I'm pullin' your leg." He took off across the field at a run, Phee barking happily as she chased him.

"Hey!" I called out. "Don't you run away from me!"

CHAPTER 13

The next day, Lucy didn't come back.

Opening the shop, I sat behind the counter, mentally preparing myself for a day manning the trenches on my own. Taking out the tarot cards, I shuffled, staring out the window at the murky day beyond.

A misty rain was falling, the kind of rain that blew in all directions and was so fine it did nothing but annoy the shite out of everyone it touched.

The bell above the door rang merrily as Boone appeared. He stamped his feet on the mat inside the door and was an inch away from shaking himself off like he was in his fox form when I held up my finger.

"Don't think about it!"

He smirked and crossed the shop, his coat all dewy with itty-bitty droplets of rain.

"She didn't show up?" he asked, leaning on the counter.

"No, she's over there with her invisibility cloak on."

"Ah, the rain's gettin' to you too, huh?" He smiled and

rubbed his hand over mine, then gestured to the tarot cards. "Have you drawn a card?"

"No. Not for a while," I replied. "I'm not sure I can handle another ominous warning."

"It might be good."

Boone was trying to cheer me up, but I was so deep in the doldrums I couldn't see a way out. Everything seemed so pointless. The fight, the whole destiny thing, even learning how to use my magic felt like a waste of time.

"The thing is, I know trouble is coming. It's always looming, you know? I don't even know how Aileen put up with it, not knowing when or where it might strike. Pretending to care about a world that didn't care about her."

"I don't think that's true," he murmured. "It's not about bein' liked."

"Then what is it about?"

"Sometimes, you need to be somethin' people hate in order to save them," he said.

"I'm not sure I can be that person," I muttered. "I want people to like me, Boone. I want to belong."

He smiled but didn't give me the reply I knew was coming. *Sometimes, we don't get to belong, even though we long for it.*

"Will you draw a card?" he asked.

I shuffled the deck once more, tempted to see what message was waiting for me, but I ended up setting the cards back into their box. If the Three of Swords showed up again, I might've spontaneously combusted.

"No," I said, putting the box under the counter. "I'm not strong enough for that today. Maybe tomorrow."

Outside, a white flash streaked past the window, signaling the arrival of the first bus for the day.

"If you need anythin', I'll be at Mary's until early afternoon, then at Molly McCreedy's."

"Sure."

Boone smiled and kissed me softly on the lips.

"Don't worry too much about Lucy," he added. "She'll turn up, or she won't."

I grunted.

"I love you," he added, backing toward the door.

Sighing, I managed a half-smile. "Love you, too."

By the time closing rolled around, the store was in chaos.

Locking the door, I turned to the mess and sighed. Starting at the closest display, I began straightening the agate slices and polishing off grubby fingerprints. Since I'd learned more about crystals and magic, I knew they absorbed energies as well as giving them out, so after a day of being handled by various strangers, they soon became muddled. I felt it every time I wrapped up a pretty specimen, so I made sure to cleanse as I went.

Picking up a slice of blue agate, I studied the pattern—which looked like the age rings in a tree trunk—and sighed. Ever since Lucy told me about the witches disliking me, I was miserable. I had no idea what I was supposed to do. Should I sit back and keep to my own—my own being Derrydun and no one else—or continue on my path to handing Carman her ass despite how my own people felt about me?

The sound of the lock turning caught my attention, and I glanced up to find Lucy pushing the door open. I could feel the hum of her magic in the air, and it made my stomach turn.

"Be careful with that," I said, putting down the agate. "I don't want your magic attracting a craglorn. I've got enough to deal with without cleaning up your mess."

"You're still angry," she said nervously.

"I'm livid!"

She glanced over her shoulder, likely regretting coming back at all. Or she was making sure she wasn't standing in the crosshairs of the sniper she'd arranged earlier.

"Do you want this job?" I asked. "Do you genuinely want it, or was it all about canvassing the village for optimal vantage points to take me out?"

"I didn't want you to find out this way," she began, and I rolled my eyes.

"I've heard that one before."

"I didn't tell them," she blurted. "They don't know about you yet."

"Who? Your coven?" I snorted and moved to the next shelf and began tidying it.

"Yeah…"

I wanted to ask her all sorts of questions, but my distrust was stronger than ever. To know there were other witches out there? I needed help learning how to use my magic, and especially a witch history one-oh-one class so I knew what to look for when it came to magical creatures and if they wanted to murder me or not. That would've been handy.

Finding where you belonged? It was meant to be a happy occasion like meeting your long-lost family, but *no*. Not for me. I was apparently the outcast.

Glancing at Lucy, who hadn't moved or uttered another word, I said, "Answer one simple question, and depending on your answer, you get to keep your job."

She nodded.

"Why did you come here? Why did you come searching for me, and why did you stay?"

"I… I wanted to see if it was true," she said. "That the Crescents were no more."

"My mother hid me well, I see," I drawled. "I suppose you had dealings with her since you seemed to know she was hanging around?"

She nodded but didn't say anything else. I figured they'd had the same amount of respect for Aileen as they now showed me, which was why she kept to herself here in Derrydun. I would have to ask Boone about it later and see what he knew because he'd never met any other witches in the whole time he'd been here, either. It was very telling.

"So the Crescents saved all your asses from Carman by kicking her out of Ireland, then closed the doorways to the fae realm," I declared, rattling off what I supposed was common knowledge. "They bound all this with their blood, *my blood*, and it's the only thing that can undo it all. Sound about right?"

Lucy blinked, looking a little shell-shocked.

"Now you're all in ultimate dilemma mode because here's the last Crescent, some random Australian chick who doesn't know shite all, who's the key to one of two things. Salvation or extinction." I raised my eyebrows. "Right?"

"Right."

"And you all hate my guts by default. Without even meeting me. Without even giving me a chance."

"It's not like that…"

"It's totally like that," I declared. "Why should I risk my life, huh? If the witches don't care about me, then maybe I should just let the fae continue hunting you all down. I'll get my powers bound again and go sip a mai tai on a beach in Thailand while you deal with your war."

They weren't fighting, so why should I? I knew there was a metaphor for survival and the human condition or something equally as poignant, but I didn't really want to think about it. Here I was thinking having magical powers would be the best thing that happened to me, like that kid and his wizarding school, owls, adventures with his two best mates, and crazy broomstick-riding classes. Instead, here I was being slammed with rotten tomatoes.

"We can't stop you," Lucy said after a moment. "If that's what you want to do, then…"

I stared at her, the gravity of who I was beginning to sink in. "You're telling me that…" I couldn't finish the sentence.

"You have more magic in you than any of us," she went on, shaking her head. "At least, of the witches I've met. Which hasn't been many."

"I'm not…" I almost choked. "I'm not all powerful. I'm just a woman…"

"You're a Crescent." She shrugged.

I narrowed my eyes and turned away, feeling really uncomfortable. Clueless Skye Williams, the savior of Ireland. *Pfft.*

Not even six months had passed since Aileen died, and I'd been a practicing witch less than that. I didn't know who to trust other than Boone, but I couldn't deny I needed help. I was a stranger to these people and to my destiny. I had no choice but to trust Lucy at least a little.

"What now?" I asked. "Now we both know the truth of our positions, what are you planning to do?"

"Me?" She raised her eyebrows. "What are you plannin'?"

"You're in my house," I shot back. "And I asked first."

"If you want to fight, then I'm obligated."

"I don't want your obligation. You may as well slap me in the face." I pouted and shook my hair. "I need a friend, Lucy. I need an ally who wants to be here because they genuinely care, not because they were conscripted against their will. If that's what you think this is, then you know where the door is. I can beat Carman with or without your help."

Her eyes seemed to light up, and she smiled. Looked like I'd said the right thing, but it was the truth. I'd always planned on facing Carman even before learning about the scandalous reputation of my coven. She'd messed with my life and loved ones, and there was no way I was going to turn a blind eye like a coward. Through Hannah the spriggan, she'd killed my mother and hurt Boone. Then there was all that crazy prophecy shite. There was no way I was letting that scrag use me!

"Then I'm with you," Lucy said.

"You can stay, on one condition."

"Anythin'."

"You must keep my existence a secret even from your coven. The Crescents are no more, you hear me? The last thing I need is random witches turning up on assassination missions. Or an influx of magic putting the village at risk. This stays between you and me. I've got enough crazy to deal with already."

"Of course."

"We don't use magic here," I said, feeling a sharp pang of protectiveness over the village. "We only use it to protect ourselves and nothing more. The hawthorns here are my birthright, and they belong to the Crescents. Got it?"

Lucy nodded.

"Say it, so I know you understand."

"Got it."

"Good." I eyed her warily and grunted.

We fell into an awkward silence, a crumbled wall of distrust still between us. Lucy began straightening the stock in the display cabinet beside me, and we rotated around the entire store before she worked up the courage to speak.

"I've got a lot of work to do, haven't I?"

"*Yep*," I said, popping the *p* at the end.

"You said you've only known you're a witch for four months?"

"Four months, yes."

"Have you had anyone show you how to use your magic?" She coughed and glanced at me. "Properly, I mean. Control and all of that."

"I've done just fine all by myself," I said haughtily.

"I can show you," she said excitedly. "I can show you how. I would love to see Crescent magic…"

It was everything I'd longed for. A teacher and a way to link to what I was. So many times I'd over juiced spells— like the mess with the craglorn—and wasn't sure how to reel it in, although I was improving. Lucy could help me, though something told me to keep my cards close to my chest and not reveal too much. About Boone, the spell book, the Crescent athame, and the visions the hawthorn in the forest tried to shove into my mind.

Speaking of the visions, I hadn't told anyone about those. Not even Boone. In all the chaos, I'd forgotten the hawthorn had tried to connect with me. Sighing, I put it on the back burner for now. That day wasn't one I wanted to remember anytime soon.

"Maybe you can show me something," I said slowly, focusing on the witch.

"Cool." Lucy beamed and finished tidying the counter. "Just name the time and place. Whenever you're ready."

And so, an uneasy alliance between a rogue witch and the last Crescent was forged. For better or worse, there was no going back now.

CHAPTER 14

I rish Moon was frosty in the days following Lucy's big reveal.

Our conversations were clipped, and the heater did nothing to warm my icy fingers. I took to wearing a pair of fingerless gloves I'd picked up from the handicraft store next door. They were made from one hundred percent Derrydun yarn, lovingly knitted by Aoife, a lady who lived out past Slieveward Bog who'd become a local celebrity when she'd found an ancient wheel of cheese that someone had buried in the sludge. I knew people liked old and moldy dairy products, but two hundred years was a bit of a stretch. Boone said the bogs were called 'nature's refrigerators,' and people used to keep all kinds of stuff in them for safekeeping, so much so, there was always a story in the local paper about the latest find. Money, jewelry, ancient swords, food, animals, and even mummified human bodies had been excavated.

The point was, Aoife, the ancient cheese lady, knitted a mean pair of fingerless gloves.

It took me a few days to get over my beaten pride

where Lucy was concerned. When it became clear she was neither going to leave me in the lurch at the shop or lead a lynch mob with flaming torches and pitchforks down the main street, I decided to cut her some slack.

I decided to close Irish Moon for the day so we could start working on the introductory crash course known as witch one-oh-one.

We bundled up in our coats, Lucy in her woolen overcoat and me in my leather jacket and scarf. We looked as different as night and day with our fashion choices. Lucy was the typical Wiccan witch, and I was the biker chick looking to rumble…all I needed was a length of chain and a skull to crack.

Lucy questioned me on what I knew as we went, using big confusing words that made me feel inadequate. She'd spent her whole life being taught how to harness and use her magic, and here I was just taking a stab in the dark with the greatest power to ever walk the earth. *No biggie*.

"Didn't the Crescents have a grimoire?" she asked, starting to weave onto shaky ground.

"If they did, I haven't found it," I replied, blatantly lying about the spell book that had become a favorite of mine.

It wasn't like I wanted to lie, but after everything that had happened with Alex and Boone, I'd learned the hard and fast rule about who to trust. Luckily, it hadn't come to anything too dire. Otherwise, I probably would've turfed Lucy out on her backside when I found her juggling crystals. This whole world was like a house of mirrors at the local carnival.

"Aileen never left you anythin' of the Crescents?"

"Other than this gnarly magic thing, no." I shook my

head. "I learned about it by accident just like everything else in my life lately."

"How did you find out?"

"You know Sean McKinnon?"

"The drunk guy from Molly McCreedy's?"

"That's the one." I snorted. "I found him drunk in a gutter one night. Completely inconsolable, mind you. I accidentally used my magic to calm him. Luckily, he was out of it. Otherwise, I don't know how I would've explained myself."

It was true, it was the first time I'd used my magic, but it wasn't exactly how I found out I was a witch. Not quite.

Lucy frowned. "So you've been alone this whole time? You know a lot…"

"I've had to learn fast. And some strange things have happened…"

Oh, man, there were so many holes in my story it wasn't funny. How could I keep Boone out of this when she kept asking a million and one things about verifying my whereabouts on x date? She was so good cop, bad cop.

"Carman and the craglorn…" She eyed me suspiciously.

"My stupid experiments caused one to come looking," I said, my hole just getting deeper and deeper. I shuddered, remembering the teeth and claws.

"You're a natural." Her skepticism was palpable.

"When you're born to fulfill a magical density, fate has a way of making things really bloody clear. Technicolor has nothing on witches and their prophecies."

"Prophecies?" Lucy asked, her head tilting to the side. "You asked me about that the other day."

"I don't really want to talk about it."

Thinking about Fae-Alex, I suppressed another

shudder. She'd warned me about him, that she felt he had malicious intent. Now I knew the truth about her, it was a lot clearer. She suspected he was a fae, but like me, she couldn't see his true face. The more I learned about this crazy-ass world, the more I knew that I'd only seen him for what he truly was because he'd attempted to use his magic on me. Magic had broken the veil.

"You sensed something was off about Alex, didn't you?" I asked, glancing at the witch.

"Yeah."

"I killed him, but I think you know that."

"I'm sorry," she said uncomfortably.

"It wasn't him. Not really. The fae had stolen his face."

We fell silent. The only sound was our boots crunching on the path beneath our feet. The forest canopy stretched overhead, blocking out most of the early morning mist. It was days like today that I wished the Crescent Witches had built an indoor amphitheater with central heating.

"Is there a spell that warms your hands?" I asked. "You know, like those little hand warmer thing you sit in your pockets that have the little buttons you click? The stuff inside crystallizes and goes hard, and then you have to boil them to reset the liquid. Is there a work around for that?"

"You're lucky I came along when I did," Lucy said with a laugh. "You're not supposed to use magic like that."

"*Damn*," I cursed. "So can I have an automated magical house like the Weasley's out of *Harry Potter*? I really wanted a pair of self-knitting needles. I've never had the attention span to knit a scarf let alone a jumper."

"Magic is supposed to augment life, not replace it," she went on.

"What does that mean?"

"No quick fixes."

"Typical."

The hawthorn came into view, and I immediately felt the pull of the tree. Since the day Boone and I had argued under her branches, its tendrils seemed to have become stronger. I knew it had to do with the connection it had made with me in my despair. I'd called out to my ancestors in a moment of desperation, and they'd tried to answer. At least, I think they did. I could've been delirious.

Finding a decent spot in the middle of the clearing, Lucy unfurled the rug she'd brought along and lay it over the dirt. She sat squarely in the middle, leaving me the edge.

"I should've brought a sandwich," I muttered. "And a thermos. A thermos would've been good. Hot chocolate."

"The first thing you should know is magic is a part of you," Lucy declared. "It's your energy you're usin', so be careful with it. Too much and you could be in serious trouble."

"I do feel tired after…" I said, the ruse not sitting right even though she was hogging the blanket in a passive-aggressive power play.

I already knew about the transference of power—it sounded all scientific and tangible that way, so that was what I was calling it. Healing Boone after he'd been attacked by the craglorn had sent me to sleep for three days with an awful fever.

"What about potions and pentagrams and all of that?" I asked. "Is that a thing?"

"Fallacy. Well, mostly."

"So I don't need to say blessed be all the time?"

"No." She giggled, smoothing her wild hair behind her ears. "You don't always need an incantation or an effigy to practice magic," she went on, giving me an overview of the basics. "There are tools we can use to aid us, but a true master needs none."

"So all the herbs, roots, and gnarly poems are optional?"

"It depends." Lucy laughed and nodded. "Unless the spell is complicated, then there's no way around it. Potions are a thing, but it's not like you see on television."

Thinking about the web I'd cast to trap the craglorn, I nodded. That was an exception to the rule. I'd had to anchor the spell to set the perimeters. This witch business wasn't all it seemed. There were so many nuances it was hard to keep up.

"Sometimes, witches use incantations to better control the spell, or they use them to center themselves. It can help keep focus if they're not good at instinctual magic."

"So are there any grand master of witches?" I asked. "You said true masters need no physical aids, but then you mentioned complicated spells needing them. Is there someone like that? Like a Jedi master?"

"No, not that I know of. I don't think there ever has been, to be honest. It's certainly possible, but it would take more than a lifetime to learn all there is to know about witchcraft."

"So it's about the path, not the destination?"

"Exactly."

"It's so philosophical."

Making a face, I flopped back onto my back and stared up at the branches of the hawthorn. I bet Carman had enough time to perfect her craft…unlike me. A thousand years compared to four months' worth of fumbling in the dark. *Whoopee.*

"All I need right now is to find a way to stop Carman," I said, voicing my concerns.

"Sure, but everythin' else is important, too."

"All that other stuff can come later. Preferably when I'm not dead."

"It's also about handlin' the amount of power rushin' through you," she scolded. "I know that even with your lack of skill, you're more powerful than me, but you need to slow down. You might think that it's kids' stuff, but you can't dive headfirst into a battle with a witch like her. Your magic could overwhelm you, and before you know it…" She raised an eyebrow.

Before I knew it, I would be a lifeless husk.

"Yeah, I know…" I sat up and started picking leaves out of my hair.

"You're arrogant," she said with a pout.

"Hang on! I never said—"

"Bein' a witch is a lifelong commitment. It's who you are. You can't just pick and choose. There are rules."

"It's who I've been for the last four months," I shot back. "There's twenty-seven years of normalcy in there, don't forget."

"Still not an excuse."

"Then show me," I said, gesturing at her. "Show me what a real witch looks like."

"A real witch knows restraint…and to not bite when baited."

I rolled my eyes, knowing she was right. I was being too hasty, and being a right pain in the rump, to boot. I was desperate to arm myself in the face of the prophecy and the little devil on my shoulder named Carman, and boy, was it showing.

"I know you're not tellin' me everythin'," Lucy said, making me pause. "And that's okay. I know I didn't give you much reason to trust me, Skye, but I will. You'll see."

I nodded. "Then let's slow down and start again. At the beginning. Show me the kids' stuff. Play dough, paper scissors, and all."

Lucy smiled and nodded. "Lesson one. Meditation."

I groaned, and my head flopped forward. "Is it playtime yet?"

"Patience, grasshopper."

CHAPTER 15

Lazing back in the floral armchair, I kicked my feet up onto the footstool and reached for another chocolate biscuit.

"You've eaten the whole packet," Boone said, giving me the evil eye from across the room.

"So?" I raised an eyebrow. "You worried I'm going to get fat? Because I'm not. They say the first place you put on weight is your hips, ass, and boobs. I wouldn't mind bigger boobs."

"Who's they?"

He glanced at my chest, and I looked at him pointedly. "*People.*"

"It's unhealthy to eat so many at once."

"See this?" I held up my hand. "Talk to it."

Turning back to the spell book, I ignored his pouting—he was totally annoyed I'd eaten all the biscuits before he could get one—and read over the page I was learning. Studying was a much easier task now I knew some of the basics. Thanks to Lucy, her crash course had unlocked some new pathways for me to explore.

One thing was becoming clearer as more pieces of the puzzle slotted into place. I'd been lucky with the magic I'd used so far. *Super lucky.* I couldn't rely on the hawthorns or the Crescent legacy to carry me through the fight to come. Besieged on all sides...

A knock at the door startled me out of my reverie, and I sat up straight, and Boone lifted his head. Who would be calling at this hour?

The knocking intensified, and I shook myself off and answered it. Flinging open the door with a scowl, my expression faded into shock as I saw who it was.

"*Mairead?*" My mouth fell open.

The Goth girl was standing on the welcome mat, looking disheveled and panicked, a large suitcase beside her. Her clothes were rumpled, and there was blood on her hand when she lifted it to try to smooth her tangled hair back into place. But it was the fear in her eyes that chilled me to the bone.

"Skye," she blurted. "I've got to warn you..."

I frowned and ushered her inside, dragging her suitcase into the hall behind us.

"What happened to you?" I asked as I closed the door, making sure it was locked.

Boone appeared in the hall, alarmed at the sight of the Goth girl.

"Mairead," he said. "You look white as a sheet."

"What are you doing here?" I went on, rubbing my hands up and down her arms. "Why aren't you in Dublin?"

"They thought I was you!" she exclaimed, holding up the talisman I'd made for her. "*They thought I was you!* Why would they think that?"

I glanced at Boone, and so did Mairead, stopping in

her tracks. Something bad had happened, and it had everything to do with my being a Crescent.

"Whatever you have to say, you can say it to both of us," I coaxed.

"They said you're a witch," she went on, starting to babble. "They wanted to drain my… I mean *your* power and take your blood."

My frown deepened, and I ushered her into the lounge room. Making her sit on the couch, I draped the throw rug over her shoulders and sat beside her.

"Slow down, and take a deep breath," I murmured. "Tell us what happened. Don't rush, you're safe here."

She sucked in a huge lungful of air, then let it out, her gaze focusing on Boone, then back to me.

"I was walkin' back to the dorm after goin' out," she began. "The city is busy, so I don't worry about walkin' at night. I was walkin', and a van pulled up beside me. I didn't even see it until it was there…"

I glanced at Boone. It might've been a glamour like the one Fae-Alex had used to hide his true face, or she may have genuinely not seen it.

"Two men jumped out…" She hesitated, then went on. "I don't know what happened after that. The next thing I remember, I was tied to a chair in a dark room."

Oh, God…

"The men were there… They said something about a ritual, and they took me blood…" She held up her hand where an angry-looking gash split across her palm. "It mustn't have worked because they came back and were really angry. They…" She sniffed. "They argued about what to do with me. One wanted to kill me and throw me in the Liffey."

I glanced at Boone.

"The river," he said.

"The other one didn't want the trouble, so they decided to cast a spell on me."

"What did they do?" I asked gently when she stalled.

"They thought they'd wiped me memory, but it didn't work. So I pretended…" She was on the verge of tears, her fist clutching around the talisman for dear life. "I pretended, and they dumped me on the street outside the dorm."

"Oh, Mairead…" I wrapped my arms around her, and she fell against my chest and started to sob. "Did they hurt you anywhere else?"

"N-no."

It must've been the talisman that made them think she was me. We looked similar, and she was carrying an identical necklace that was imbued with Crescent magic. It got her into trouble, but when it counted, it had saved her from having her memory wiped clean. Who knew what their intent was? She could be a mindless shell right about now—or worse…floating facedown in a river.

"Boone?"

"Yeah?" He snapped to attention.

"Could you make Mairead a hot cup of tea? And there are chocolate biscuits in the top cupboard."

He nodded—not giving me any lip about my secret stash of biscuits—and glanced at her once more before stomping into the kitchen.

"I won't lie to you, Mairead," I said once we were alone. "I've dropped you into the middle of a war without meaning to. There are people and *things* out there that want me dead, all because of what I am and what I can do. I'm so sorry. I never meant for you to be dragged into this. I wanted to protect you."

"It's true?" Her eyes sparkled with tears, and her skin was puffy.

"It's true."

"You can do magic? Actual magic?"

"Yep. Freaks me out, too."

She sniffed and wiped at her eyes, pulling away from me. Opening her palm, she stared at the crystal.

"I made it to protect you," I said. "See those gold flecks? That's the color of my magic."

"Really?"

I nodded. "I'm sorry I got you into trouble."

"They wanted to hurt you, Skye. Whatever they wanted it sounded bad."

I didn't want to be reminded of the prophecy, but here it was in all its gory glory. It was time to sit up and start paying attention. The war the Crescents had been waiting a thousand years to come to blows was finally here, and the enemy had made the first move. I had to up my game and fast.

"Here," I said, gesturing for Mairead's injured hand. "Let me see."

She held out her hand and rested it gingerly in mine. Closing my opposite hand over hers, I focused my magic. Feeling the warm golden glow in my stomach, I nudged it into the cut. Since we were away from the hawthorn, it was only a trickle, but it was enough that Boone reappeared.

"Skye…"

"*Shh*," I said. "Let me do this."

Imagining Mairead's skin growing and joining, I finally felt the magic cease as the spell ran its course. Removing my hand from hers, I smiled when I saw the cut was completely healed. She needed a bar of soap, but that was trivial.

"*Oh mo dhia,*" she whispered, staring at her hand.

"Good as new," I declared, rather pleased with myself. This magic thing was getting easier the more I practiced. Boone was right about the instinctual thing, but I'd had a hard time connecting the two things together until now. Magic and intent.

"Was Aileen like you, too?"

"Yes, she was."

"That explains so much…" she mused.

"Do your parents know where you are?" I went on. "Do they know what happened?"

"Don't tell them!" she exclaimed.

"They need to know you're not at school," I countered. "But the magic and the kidnapping thing…"

I didn't like it, but we had to keep it a secret. The police couldn't do anything against Carman and her agents, neither could Mairead's mum or dad. Telling them and making a fuss would only expose all of us, and then we'd all be locked up in some government facility where we would be cut open and experimented on. That would be a real hoot. I wondered what the food was like…

"You can't tell anyone about this, Mairead," Boone said, kneeling before the girl. "Magic is dyin', and Skye is the only one who can stop it. If somethin' happens to her, then I don't know what'll happen to the rest of us. And that's only the beginnin' of it."

"Way to alarm the girl," I declared, but Mairead nodded.

"I know," she said. "I figured since people don't believe and all."

"We have to figure out something," I mused aloud.

"I can't go back," she exclaimed, grasping my arm. "I can't go back there."

"We'll figure it out," I said.

"Skye, I'm afraid."

It was the most genuine I'd ever seen Mairead. Usually, she was aloof and did whatever she could to hide her emotions, but in the wake of her ordeal, her mask was gone. Underneath, she was just an eighteen-year-old girl with the same hopes, fears, and dreams as everyone else. I was all for individuality, but at our core, we all had the same feelings.

"Will they come here?" she asked fretfully.

"No. We're protected here," I replied. "The hawthorn trees shield us from the bad guys, I've got a magical dagger, and we have Boone."

Mairead glanced at him and frowned. "Are you…"

"Nay," he said, shaking his head. "I'm somethin' else entirely." He'd returned with the tea and biscuits and set them on the coffee table.

"Here," I said, handing her the cup of tea. "Have this and a couple of chocolate bickies. It'll warm you up, and a sugar hit never hurt anyone."

Standing, I gestured for Boone to follow me into the kitchen so we could talk.

"What a mess," I said.

"Aye, to be sure." He glanced back at Mairead, clearly worried.

"It's the prophecy," I whispered. "It's coming true. *The spell will be broken. The blood of the golden one will crack the chains, and she will return.*"

"It's only true if they manage to take the right person," he replied. "We thought they might try somethin' like this."

"Yeah, but not against Mairead!" I seethed and began grinding my teeth.

"Calm down," Boone murmured. "She's all right,

Skye. While she's with us, they won't be able to touch her again. The hawthorns will protect her."

"They shouldn't have touched her in the first place. Did you see how scared she is?" I jabbed a finger toward the lounge room. "All because I gave her that talisman."

"You couldn't have known. You were tryin' to help."

"I feel like I shouldn't have." I rubbed my eyes, the weight on my shoulders feeling heavier than ever.

Boone wrapped his arms around me and squeezed. His touch was reassuring, but I couldn't shake Mairead's expression.

I shook my head. "It's happening. I didn't think it would be so soon…"

"It'll be all right."

"Carman is already trying to sink her claws into me," I went on. "She knows I'm here, and she knows I'm the last. She has to if she was brazen enough to snatch Mairead off the street."

"There's no way she could know how powerful you are," Boone said. "You need to mask your magic until the right moment."

I nodded, glancing back to where Mairead was sipping her tea.

"When you unleashed on that craglorn," Boone whispered into my ear. "It was incredible. You were brighter than Aileen. I know it's a big ask, fightin' for us, especially after what Lucy told you about the witches, but I believe in you. And now so does Mairead. Did you see the look in her eyes when you healed her hand? That girl idolizes you."

I snorted. "It's hard to take the high road when I don't know what I'm doing."

"Neither of us chose our paths, Skye, but we're on them all the same."

Boone was always right. I didn't know why I fought against him anymore. It was just my own insecurities talking, and the fear of the unknown. I suppose that was how I knew I was human.

I untangled myself from Boone's arms and straightened my jumper. "Right. I better get Mairead set up in the spare room."

He let me go, but I felt his eyes on my back. I could wield my sword of sass all I wanted, but when it came down to the crunch, my one-liners wouldn't save me. It was time to grow up. *Hashtag adulting.*

Taking the empty cup of tea from Mairead, I smiled. "It's late, and you look exhausted. I have a spare bed upstairs if you want to stay."

She nodded.

"Then tomorrow, we'll figure out what to tell your parents."

"I won't tell," she exclaimed. "I won't tell anyone what happened. I promise."

"I know. I trust you."

She smiled, the color returning to her cheeks.

Standing, I coaxed her to follow. "Let's get you to bed."

As I tucked Mairead in—which was a strange sensation considering our relationship—I felt a pang of rage twisting my gut.

I'd expected Carman to go after me, what with her craglorns and trickster fae, but now she'd messed with an innocent girl. There was no way I was letting that scrag get away with it.

If I doubted my abilities before today, then I didn't

anymore. I couldn't waver. I had to believe one hundred percent. It was as simple as that.

One way or another, Carman was going to pay.

CHAPTER 16

The next morning, I took Mairead home to her parents.

I'd seen Beth and Gregory around the village from time to time, but I'd never developed a close friendship with the pair like I had with their daughter. So it came as no surprise that Mairead had run to me before she went to them.

Sitting on their couch, I nursed a cup of tea while Gregory sat in an armchair rolling his eyes while we heard the docile tones of Beth screaming her displeasure to her daughter.

There was something about dropping out of Trinity, then her fashion choices, and squandering her one chance at a decent future. I rolled my eyes, knowing plenty of people didn't know what they wanted to do at eighteen, and university wasn't a onetime deal. Mairead could always go back.

As for her fashion choices, there were worse hues out there than black. Like poo brown. And beige. Beige was pretty woeful.

"Mum!" Mairead wailed, following Beth back into the sitting room.

Gregory gave me a sympathetic look, which was a precursor to the roasting I was about to get.

"It's you McKinney's always leadin' her astray," the older woman declared.

I gasped dramatically and held my hand to my chest like I was wounded.

"You're just the same as Aileen, puttin' nonsense in her head."

"Beth, darlin'," Gregory began but was immediately shut down.

"Me daughter drops out of school in the middle of the night and goes straight to you!"

Setting down the cup and saucer, I resisted the urge to turn her into a toad with disgusting warts on her private parts.

"Mum!"

"You keep quiet, Mairead."

Gregory was silent, proving it was the women of the household who wore the pants.

"If she won't go back to Trinity, then I can't have her under me roof!" Beth exclaimed. "I can't have it!"

I could just tell them what happened to their daughter, but it would make things worse. It would blow the lid off everything and unleash something far worse than Mairead dropping out of Trinity—which was news to me.

"I'm not sitting here and taking this," I said calmly, surprising myself at my restraint. That toad was still looking rather appealing. "Mairead is welcome to take her job back at Irish Moon anytime she wants. She also has a place to stay with me. No questions asked. Life is tough, but not as tough as growing up. She needs you, but if you don't want her, then she's welcome to come with me."

Snatching up my jacket, I nodded at Gregory and stormed out the front door, Mairead on my heels. I mightn't have had Aileen growing up, but right about now, I was glad for my dad's influence. Even when I was a complete ratbag, he'd never turfed me out onto the street. Beth was such a drag, but I reckon she knew I was going to pick up the slack…which made it even worse. Dumping your parental responsibility on a twenty-eight-year-old woman with zero child-rearing experience was real smooth.

Poor Mairead.

"I can't believe Mum kicked me out," she seethed as we walked down the lane.

In the distance, I could see the spire of St. Brigid's peeking over the treetops. The sky was gray, matching both our moods as we walked back toward Derrydun and Irish Moon.

"Do you really want to drop out of university?" I asked.

"I can't go back there."

"I know you went through a horrible situation, but it's not just about that. It's also about your future."

She shrugged, rolling her eyes. It was a classic avoidance tactic and one I was well versed in, what with my past as a pouty teenager and all.

"We can find a way to shield you from the fae," I added. "Then you won't have to worry about all of that. You might've missed a few classes, but you can pick it back up, right?"

Mairead pouted. "So?"

"So?" I scowled, getting the vibe something else was in

play. "Mairead… Did something else happen?"

She kicked the ground, scuffing the toe of her boot against a fence as we passed.

"*Mairead.* You know my deepest, darkest secret."

"I hated it, okay!" she exclaimed, tears welling in her eyes. "I didn't fit in, the professors picked on me, and I didn't make one friend. Not one!"

"I'm sorry." My shoulders sank, and I reached out and pulled her into a hug.

"I don't want to go back. They don't want me there."

"People suck, but you can't let one asshole ruin everything for you. High school never ends, it just levels up."

She turned her head away and sniffed, then came out with the million-dollar question. "What's wrong with me?"

"Nothing," I replied. "Nothing is wrong with you."

She sniffed again, dabbing gently at her tears and trying her best not to smear her eyeliner.

"Sometimes, we just don't fit, I suppose," I went on. "It's nothing to beat yourself up over. You've just got to find where you belong. Everyone goes through it." I snorted and gestured to myself. "I'm still trying to figure it out."

"That doesn't help."

"Oh, jeez," I declared, rolling my eyes. "Cut me some slack. I'm not Yoda. That's Boone's area of expertise. I'm the hotheaded one who leaps into trouble headfirst and talks her way out of it with sass and pop culture references."

We continued walking toward Derrydun in silence.

"Did you really mean it?" Mairead asked after a while.

"Mean what?"

"That I can stay with you?"

She was looking at me hopefully, and I groaned. What had I gotten myself into?

"I have one condition," I said, waiting for her to acknowledge my demand.

She nodded.

"I reserve the right to ground you."

When we arrived at Irish Moon, it was five minutes to ten, and Lucy was waiting out the front.

Luckily for me, I'd warned Mairead about the new hire the night before and gave her the heads up to keep Boone out of our witchy conversations. Still, the Goth girl glared and pouted as I introduced the two.

"Mairead, Lucy. Lucy, Mairead."

"Ah, so you're the famous author of the Irish Moon employee handbook," Lucy declared, causing Mairead to falter.

"Yeah, that's me."

Snickering, I unlocked the door and let us in out of the cold.

"Mairead's had a little falling out with Trinity College," I explained. "She'll be back helping out around here for a while."

"Oh," Lucy said. "Does that mean…"

"You still have your job, don't worry."

The witch smiled and looked rather pleased. All this hero worship was starting to go to my head.

"And FYI, there was a slip…and an awkward moment where she found out about *you know what*."

Lucy's mouth fell open, and she glanced at me, looking alarmed.

"Ixnay on the witchy-stay." I winked at Mairead and laughed.

"It's not a joke!" the witch declared.

"And I trust Mairead implicitly." I glared at her, pulling rank. "My turf, remember?"

Lucy backed down immediately, but her distrust was clear as day.

"Things are changing," I went on, going for my tarot cards as Mairead switched on the heating. "I can feel something coming. Aileen was waiting for it, but she never got to see it. The more I learn, the more I envy her to be honest. I'm the last Crescent. There's no one else to take the mantle, so it's time. *My time.* We have to adapt…and that means a new work roster."

"That was an anticlimax," Mairead said with a groan. "I was ready to go find a sword or somethin' and dig a trench."

Opening the box of tarot cards, I laughed. "Got to make a joke sometimes. Otherwise, what a dreary bunch we would be."

Shuffling the deck, I kicked back and allowed my minions to open up the shop. Having two employees was rather liberating. I could laze about all day! What a stroke of cheeky luck.

Setting the cards on the counter, I swept them to the side, fanning out the black and gold rectangles. Eyeing the Goth girl, I got an idea.

"Hey, Mairead," I said, gesturing her to come forward. "Pick a card. *Any card.*"

"Um… I don't really know about that," she said, sheepishly eyeing the cards.

"Didn't Aileen ever draw one for you?"

"Never."

"Then considering the change in climate, go for it." I gestured to the spread. "Pick one that calls to you."

"That's it?" she asked while Lucy watched on with a smile. "Just pick one?"

"Yep." I nodded. "It's that simple."

Mairead held her hand out over the cards and moved it back and forth a few times before she plucked a card from the left-hand side of the spread. Turning it over, she scowled.

"The Fool?" she exclaimed, sounding offended. "That's the card I get?"

"Calm your farm," I said, swatting away her flailing arms. "It doesn't mean you're an idiot."

"Then what *does* it mean?"

"The Fool is a card for new beginnings, which is rather apt, don't you think?" I took the card from her and set it on the counter. Tapping it, I coaxed her to focus. "University, finding out about magic… Hmm?"

Mairead nodded and started to calm down a little.

"It means you're ready to start a new journey, one that is filled with possibility. It can sometimes mean there's a choice you need to make, so think about what it could be. Maybe about going back to Trinity, or changing your career, or about you coming back to Derrydun. Right now, I would say it's showing you the world is at your feet but to carefully consider your path. The Fool is telling you to *trust yourself*."

Mairead had fallen completely silent, and for the first time in her life, she was rendered speechless. She picked up the card and stared at it so intently I thought it might burst into flames. Glancing at Lucy, we exchanged a knowing smile.

It was exactly what she'd needed to hear.

After an eventful day at Irish Moon, Mairead and I walked back to the cottage, dead on our feet.

Everyone was surprised to see the Goth girl back behind the counter. First, Mary Donnelly made a fuss asking all sorts of questions, and then we watched her through the window as she spoke to Mrs. Boyle, then accosted Maggie as she was opening Molly McCreedy's. In T-minus five minutes, the whole village knew Mairead was back.

I had no doubt in my mind that after a good talking to from Beth, the story would morph into *that Skye Williams has been a negative influence on that young girl's mind, and look out before she casts a spell on you!* If only they knew the truth. I made a mental note to see what I could do about that toad spell or, at the least, warts on the nether region part. Imagine getting the local doctor to burn those off with dry ice.

"So, what's Boone?" Mairead asked, scowling when I put a steaming microwave meal in front of her. *I was such a good parent.*

"Boone's a shapeshifter," I replied, handing her a knife and fork.

"No way!"

"Way." I grimaced and stabbed at a soggy roast potato.

"Like a werewolf?" she asked, chattering excitedly. "Or somethin' else?"

"He's a tabby cat," I said with a smirk.

"Stop messin' with me."

I waved my fork in the air. "Next time you see Father O'Donegal's tabby cat, it mightn't be the cat but someone else, is all I'm saying."

"Stop pullin' me leg," she complained. "That's really lame. I bet he's somethin' way cooler."

"You'll just have to ask him when he gets home," I said with a cheeky smile, leaving out all the other shapes he was fond of on purpose. "But I'm not lying. He's a tabby cat."

Mairead began to sulk as she ate her dinner, originally impressed her crush had turned out to be badass…until she found his shapeshifter shape was a house cat.

"I'm going to have to work out a roster for Irish Moon," I said. "I can't leave Lucy without too much work. Nor can I kick her out just because you're back. I'm not exactly made of money."

"Now I'm here, I can mind the shop while you learn how to use your powers," she said, looking pleased with herself. "I don't mind."

"I'm not a superhero, you know."

She shrugged and smiled sweetly.

"It's not fun and games," I went on, my scowl deepening. "Or have you forgotten about the dudes looking for my blood to complete their creepy serial killer ritual?"

Mairead paled and shook her head. "Of course, I haven't forgotten. I was kidnapped and tied to a chair!"

I groaned. "Sorry. There goes my mouth again."

"I know everythin' now," she said. "You may as well explain it to me. I could help. At least with the shop."

She was right. Maybe if she knew, then she would be able to protect herself or help in some way. I didn't like her being messed up in this, but it was done now. No going back.

"There's someone who wants to get back into Ireland," I explained. "She was kicked out a long time ago and is majorly pissed."

"Who?"

"A witch named Carman."

Mairead made a face. "Carman from the myth?"

"I suppose so."

"In Irish mythology, during the time of the Tuatha Dé Danann, Ireland was invaded by a Celtic Witch named Carman," Mairead rattled off, signaling she'd learned something at university after all. "She was a Greek warrior who invaded with her three sons. They had destroyed all of Ireland's crops before they were stopped. You're talkin' about that Carman?"

"She had three sons?" I made a face and rolled my eyes. "*Great.* No one told me about the demon spawn."

"I dunno." Mairead snorted. "It's just a story. What does she want anyway?"

"She's stealing magic and saving it up so she can unlock the doorways to the fae realm," I replied. "Probably so she can lay waste to Ireland again."

"The fae realm?"

I nodded. "Sounds completely bonkers, but it's the truth. The doors were shut a long time ago, and people from both sides were stuck. Fae were trapped here, and magical human types were trapped there. She's stealing magic, but there are things here that need it to survive, too. Things that have become evil and twisted. That's why we need to be careful using our magic. We're being hunted on all sides."

"What happens if she opens the doors?" Mairead asked, her eyes wide.

"That's the fifty-million-billion-trillion-dollar question. Anything could happen. Armageddon or sunshine and rainbows. No one knows, but if that story is anything to go by"—I whistled—"lucky us."

"You don't know much."

"The only thing I do know is Carman is pure evil, and the Crescent Witches—that's me—were the only ones powerful enough to stand up to her. That's why they need my blood, and I'm the only one in her way. There was a reason she was cursed out of Ireland, and there was a reason the fae realm was sealed from ours. Somehow, I don't think it was to do with razing crops. The stories don't seem to mention that part."

"What reason?"

"You ask a lot of questions, you know that?"

"That means you don't know," she said with a pout.

"No, I don't. I didn't even know I was a witch until I saw—" I stopped dead in my tracks, not wanting to tell Mairead of all people about the time I found Boone naked on the end of my bed.

"Saw what?"

"Nothing."

She eyed me skeptically.

"The myths say Carman died," she declared. "And when she did, a festival was named after her. It was called *Óenach Carmain*. There's a similar festival that's still held now. *Lughnasadh*. There are tons of different myths about different goddesses and stuff. I guess it depends on who you're talkin' to."

"What's that?" I asked, another Irish thing going straight over my head.

"*Lughnasadh* is like a giant farmer's market. There's food, animals, craft markets, and stuff. It's a Wiccan harvest festival."

"So you did learn something at university," I declared. "Ha!"

"Maybe…"

Thinking of what Mairead said about the myth surrounding Carman, I began to wonder what her endgame was the first time around. She'd destroyed Ireland's crops, taking out the food source and causing havoc until the Crescent Witches stopped her. But there was one flaw in the history books. Carman wasn't dead.

The door opened then slammed closed, and Boone appeared.

Mairead smiled, instantly brightening at the sight of him.

"Don't get any ideas," I said. "I haven't forgotten the time when you conned him into giving you a kiss."

"Are you really a tabby cat?" she demanded.

Boone glanced at me and chuckled. "You've been tellin' her stories."

"I left out the good bits."

"What good bits?" Mairead wailed.

Watching Boone as he filled the girl in on his abilities and his memory loss, a feeling of warmth spread through my chest. It felt good to be able to tell someone about all of this. Keeping a secret was hard work.

Thinking about crazy Beth and her pushover of a husband, Gregory, I sighed. It had been a pain in my ass knowing the witches weren't a fan, and it looked like humanity was jumping onto the bandwagon.

And so, the existential question of the century kept coming around and around, haunting my every move. Why should I lift a finger to help? *If only they knew what was waiting for them.*

Focusing on Boone and Mairead's conversation, I knew I would fight, anyway. First, for them, and then time would tell if it would be for everyone else.

CHAPTER 17

"Skye." A hand shook my shoulder. "Are you awake?"

"It's Saturday, Dad," I said, moaning and swatting blindly. "Let me sleep in."

"*Skye.*"

The shaking intensified, and my head snapped up. Mairead was crouched beside the bed, dressed in her nightie, her eyes wide.

"What? What's wrong?" I asked, reaching for the lamp.

Warm light illuminated the room. Luckily, Boone had gone home, and we weren't in the middle of sexy times. Otherwise, I would've been mortified.

"I..." She glanced at the bed and shivered, her bare toes twitching.

"Did you have a bad dream?"

She nodded.

"Get in." Rolling over, I rubbed my eyes and patted the bed next to me.

Mairead scrambled around the end of the bed and slid in next to me.

"You want to talk about it?" I asked, facing her.

"It was just about the… You know." She buried under the covers, hiding her face.

"I'm sorry… You've been handling things really well. Like a boss, actually."

"I feel better with you and Boone around."

I smiled, though I felt a pang stab me in the chest at another reminder of my responsibility. I wondered how Aileen had handled it.

"I guess it just hit me," she went on, her fingers worrying the edge of the quilt. "I could've died." She sniffed, her eyes misting with tears.

"It's okay," I murmured.

"I thought about it, about what you have to do—and what Aileen was doin' for us—and it must be hard. You're riskin' your life."

"Hey, don't worry about me," I said. "I'm working on it. Which makes me wonder about you."

"Why?"

"Have you thought about what you want to do with Trinity?"

Mairead made a face.

"Maybe you were taking the wrong classes," I suggested. "What were you studying?"

"Psychology."

I remembered when I was in high school psychology seemed to be the buzzword of all the seniors. Like fleek, and YOLO, or whatever the kids nowadays were saying. Psychology had been the career choice of the moment.

"Is that something you want to do? Or was it something you chose because you had to choose something? I know how these high school career councilors work. Not everyone has their life mapped out at seventeen."

"I'm eighteen."

"Are you?"

"Me birthday was last month." She pouted.

"Did I say happy birthday?"

"No."

"Not even on Facebook?"

"*No.*"

"Then I'll make it up to you." I thought for a moment. "What was I doing last month? Oh, yeah, I was battling the mind manipulation of a fae who'd stolen the identity of my ex-boyfriend."

Mairead screwed her nose. "Huh?"

"It's a long story, but we were talking about you and your gnarly dream."

"Do you think it's stress?" she asked.

"Honestly, I think it's more about the kidnapping part."

"Skye, I… I'm tryin'. I want to be strong."

"I know. I can tell."

We fell silent, listening to the night outside. All was still, which meant, tomorrow, frost would be lying on the ground, coating everything in a thin sheen of white droplets.

"I don't want to be a psychologist," Mairead blurted.

I smiled. "I know."

"Then why didn't you tell me!"

"It's not about me," I said. "Anyway, it wouldn't have been your choice if I told you." And just like that, all this witchy business about the journey, not the destination, smacked me directly in the face. Looked like we both had a lightbulb moment.

Damn, I was growing up and being all responsible and stuff.

"What do you like doing?" I went on. "You must have

some idea you've disregarded because it's frivolous. Don't forget, we live in the age of the Internet. It's a good time for small business. Just look at Irish Moon."

"You should open an online shop."

"Hey, now there's… *Mairead!* Don't change the subject."

She thought, her forehead screwing up.

"It's two a.m.," I complained, winding her up. "Let's go back to sleep…"

"I like to draw, okay," she declared.

"You draw?" I raised my eyebrows. "Cool."

"Who ever made a job out of drawing?" She pouted.

"Plenty of people. Ever hear of the comic book industry?"

Her scowl deepened. It looked like she'd already forgotten about the lesson The Fool presented. Luckily, she had me to give her a kick up the rear end.

"Then I'll make you a deal," I said. "Tomorrow, start working on your drawings, and I'll help you brainstorm."

"Brainstorm?"

"Time to hustle, Mairead. We've both got destinies to fulfill." I gave her a look, then reached for the lamp. "Can I go to sleep now? I get angry when I'm tired."

She nodded. "Yeah."

The room was plunged into darkness, and I nestled back into bed, my head finding the groove in my pillow.

"Hey, Skye?" Mairead whispered.

"Yeah?"

"Are you scared?"

I hesitated and looked inward for my truth. Lucy was right about my arrogance, but I was beginning to believe it was to do with fear more than ego, especially after Mairead's near miss. Which meant, I still had time to learn how to be humble. *With great power comes great responsibility*, or so the saying from Spiderman went.

"Yeah," I replied. "I wouldn't be human if I wasn't a little afraid."

And so life went on much the same way for the next few weeks.

The days shortened, the temperature dropped, rain drizzled, and the mornings were fraught with fog and vaporizing breath. I'd begun wearing a gray knit beanie—another of Cheese Wheel Aoife's creations—with my fingerless gloves twenty-four seven. Those babies only came off my mitts when I went to take a whiz.

Boone had warned me about snow and sub-zero temperatures, and while I was looking forward to a real wintery Christmas, I was hoping I would still have toes by then.

Despite the cold, Irish Moon was buzzing with customers. Mairead and Lucy alternated their working schedule, fitting around each other with minimum fuss. The tourist season was beginning to wind down, and the buses were less frequent, which gave me some breathing room when it came to practicing my magic. I wasn't at the grand-master level yet, but things were starting to make a lot more sense than when I was just stabbing in the dark.

The clearing underneath the branches of the hawthorn tree was one of the most familiar places in the whole of Derrydun. Even more than the cottage was if you could believe it. I knew every rise and fall of the earth, every twist of the hawthorn's roots, every snarl in her bark, every wisp of fern around the edges of the forest, and every shadow that played across the entire scene.

I'd fought against this place for so long even after I found out I was destined to protect it. Now… Well, I don't know when it happened, but it had become home.

"So, tree," I said, gazing up at the branches. "You're the largest hawthorn there ever was and will be. You must've seen some screwed-up shite in your time, hey?" I made a face. "You must be laughing at my lackluster attempts at practicing magic. Ready for another round?"

Standing before the tree, I closed my eyes and took a deep breath, centering my mind and magic just like Lucy had taught me. I felt my power bubbling in my belly and focused on shaping it. Warmth spread to my chest, down through my legs, and then along my arms until I could feel the Crescent legacy in my entire body.

Okay, hold it there, I thought, concentrating on keeping it contained.

I held as long as I could before letting my magic go. Instead of pushing it outward, like I imagined when I was doing a spell, I let it deflate and simmer back into a dormant state. I was totally getting better at this. Control was ninety-five percent of being a witch, Lucy said.

Reaching out, I lay my palm against the trunk of the hawthorn. Another thing Lucy had confirmed was that witches had an ability to connect with the plants and earth, which explained why I could sense the spring winding its way through the ground at Croagh Patrick. Remembering the cool sensation of something rushing past me, I shivered.

"We really need to build you a greenhouse or something," I said, almost expecting the tree to answer.

Well, it had before, hadn't it?

"When I touched you last time, you tried to tell something, didn't you?" I asked, then snorted as I realized I was talking to a tree. A magical tree, but still… "And that didn't sound half dirty. Touching a tree. *Pfft.*"

Squaring my shoulders, I decided there was no harm in trying. This place had been my ancestral home for over a thousand years. I had nothing to worry about even though underneath her roots, lay the hawthorn's original purpose. Guarding a doorway to the fae realm.

I'd never really thought about it that way, and now I was pondering the notion, a prickling sensation scratched at the back of my neck, then shivered down my spine and back up again. There was a portal to another world under the tree outside Irish Moon. *Brrr!*

Shaking my head, I focused my mind and reached out toward the hawthorn. Nothing happened—at least, not straightaway.

My skin crawled as if slimy, gooey worms were slithering up my arms and legs, and I almost pulled away. At the last second, I realized it was the tree answering my call. Her tendrils were reaching out—roots, branches, and vines—to greet me.

"So you are in there," I murmured. "What were you trying to tell me, hawthorn? I don't know, but I'm glad you're here."

I was plunged into darkness before twisting and turning. I was falling like when Alice fell down the rabbit hole. Panicking, I screamed, reaching out for something to grab hold of, but there was nothing there.

I fell on my ass, the wind rushing out of my lungs, and I moaned. *Ow, my butt cheek.*

Glancing up, I almost did a little wee when I saw a face staring down at me. Not just any face. It was a tree with leaves for hair, bark for skin, and awful glowing green eyes. Boone had told me about her, about how she'd drowned Aileen in the earth. It could only be one person.

"Hannah?"

She wailed, her voice peeling with a thousand threads of pain, and the ground began to rumble beneath my feet.

"No…" I scrambled to my feet, but I was caught.

The forest floor turned to quicksand, and I sank, my boots sticking. The pressure against my legs was unbearable, and I screamed for help, but no one came. I struggled, but the more I moved, the faster I was swallowed up.

"*I'm coming,*" a voice whispered in my ear. "*Wait for me.*"

A heavy pressure was squashing my chest, causing my limbs to slow. Dirt filled my mouth, choking and stealing my breath. Struggling for air, I clawed at the earth, trying desperately to fight my way out of the darkness. Reaching toward the surface, I pushed and kicked, climbing higher and higher.

"*Skye!*"

Light burst in my eyes, and I coughed violently, spitting dirt onto the ground before me. What a rush!

Turning, I wiped the tears from my eyes and shook out the earth still clinging to my clothes. I stilled when I realized I was standing in the center of Derrydun. *How did I get here?*

Overhead, the sun was shining, and I felt sweat prickling across my forehead. It was the middle of summer, which was completely confusing. A moment ago, I'd been in the midst of the deep and dark Irish autumn.

Glancing up at the sky, I frowned at the yellowish hue that was laid over the blue. It was like I was looking through a filter labeled sepia. Turning around, I scratched my head when I saw how different the village looked.

Mary's Teahouse was still neon pink, but the Virginia creeper that grew all over Molly McCreedy's wasn't as wild. The handicrafts store had been replaced with a shop called Lush Lavender - Irish Arts & Crafts, the hawthorn tree in the middle of the road was two-thirds of the size, and Irish Moon wasn't there at all.

Crossing the street, I cupped my hands against the window and peered inside at the empty building. Without all the crystals and shop fittings, it looked so big. And empty. Did I say that already?

Where the fudge was I? Had the hawthorn transported me into another vision, or had I taken a ride in a DeLorean at eighty-eight miles per hour?

"You must be Aileen."

Turning, I gasped as I came face-to-face with Mary Donnelly. A really young looking Mary Donnelly. I mean, she was still older, but not as…*ah, forget it.*

"I'm sorry to startle you, dear," she said. "I saw you standin' there, and I wanted to offer my condolences. It's a terrible shock. Just terrible."

"That's…okay?" I replied, giving her the once-over. Eyeing her shoulder pads and sequin embellished T-shirt, I held onto my brewing giggle. And she gave Mairead grief over her fashion choices? *Hello, nineteen eighty-nine.*

"Are you interested?" Mary went on, nodding toward the shop. "It's been empty for so long. Robert thinks the tourist industry is about to boom. It could be a good investment for the right sort of person."

"Robert?" I tilted my head to the side.

"O'Keeffe," she replied. "He was at the funeral. Did you meet him?"

"The funeral?"

Mary placed her hand on my shoulder and gave me a concerned look. "Oh, dear, you've really been through the wars. It must be just awful comin' home after so long to all of this."

I was beginning to feel rather sick the longer she spoke to me. It was eerily similar to my calling. Aileen had left Dad and me when I was two. I knew the Crescent legacy was to blame, and something terrible had happened, but no one had ever spoken about it. It was almost thirty years ago.

It seemed Aileen and I were more similar than I'd ever known.

"What happened to them?" I asked.

She gave me a curious look. I was supposed to know, being in my mother's body and all, so to her, I was acting out of character even for someone overcome with grief.

"Why, they were found in the woods," she said. "Aileen, darlin'. Are you feelin' okay? Would you like to come to the teahouse for a cup of tea and a scone? My treat."

"Mary, what happened to them? Who were they?"

Her frown deepened, but she began to speak, her words gentle and considered.

"Your grandmother, mother, and aunt were found in the woods behind the village. They'd been bound..." She coughed, looking uncomfortable as the bile began rising in the back of my throat. "They were burned."

Skye.

A cold blast of air blew on the back of my neck, and I turned, my body plunging deep into the darkness of the forest.

Something rough was digging into my wrists, and I couldn't move. Struggling, I turned my head, my gaze locking with a woman my age. Black hair, green eyes, pale skin.

Movement drew my attention forward, and I swallowed a scream as I saw nothing but wild, curly hair and anger. Anger and…flame.

"Crescent *bitch*."

"Don't listen to her," the woman beside me said. "She'll come. She'll come, and you'll be sorry."

Fear, fear, fear… Then a wrenching, burning, *searing* agony and…nothing. Darkness.

I wasn't sure how long I floated. There was no direction where I was. No up, down, or side to side.

It started as a simple dot in the black. A pinprick of color began to grow, larger and larger until I realized I was looking at a flower.

It was a simple thing—a purple star with a yellow center—but I knew it was deadly when put into the right potion. Lucy had taught me about it, and I'd seen it in the pages of my spell book. Nightshade.

The image was pounded into my brain like I was being hit over and over with a sledgehammer. *Nightshade, nightshade, nightshade.*

It was a warning, but what for? Was I being poisoned? Did the flower represent something or someone?

Pain erupted in my head, and I was wrenched away from the image, light and color bursting all around me. I fell to my knees, my fingers curling in the leaf litter at the base of the hawthorn. Gasping for breath, I fought for clarity as I was struck again.

My shoulder slammed into the ground, and I fell onto my back, crying out in pain.

Someone was standing over me, holding a large

branch. My vision wavered, and I tried to push myself up, but my head was spinning.

Curly wild hair… No!

Lucy.

"I'm sorry, Skye," she said, raising the branch again.

The Three of Swords was finally playing out to its full extent. I'd forgotten all about the warning, not to mention I'd disregarded listening to the hawthorn until it was too late. *I was so stupid!*

Lucy was the third sword.

CHAPTER 18

Coming to was the strangest sensation.

It wasn't like waking up in the morning. It was like trying to swim through a darkness that had no shape or form. Almost as if my mind was trying to wade through quicksand.

My head throbbed, and I was having a hard time concentrating. This wasn't natural. Not one bit.

Moving my arms, I was met with resistance, and it took me a full minute to realize I'd been tied to something. I was lying down, but where was I?

Turning my head, I grimaced when I saw Lucy kneeling at the side of what looked like a clearing. There were trees and warm, orange lights. Torches?

Immediately, the prophecy came to mind, and I began to panic. Lucy was performing the ritual to break the curse. *The curse that kept Carman from returning to Ireland.*

I pulled at the restraints, but I was stuck fast. I was tied down with magic to a stone slab deep in the forest. Had to be.

"Strugglin' will do you no good," Lucy said without turning around.

"How could you?" I demanded.

"How could I?" She turned around and snarled. "I had no choice. Unlike you."

"Nightshade," I said with a moan, my head practically splitting in two. She must've hit me with a real wallop. "Your coven is the Nightshade Witches…"

She narrowed her eyes, her lip curling. Every scrap of friendliness she'd ever shown me was gone. Her mask had dissolved, letting out the angry and bitter witch underneath.

"Took you long enough."

"I probably never would've found out!" I exclaimed. "I'm alone, or have you forgotten? You were supposed to help me…"

"I was never *supposed* to do anythin'. Welcome to the real world, Skye, where everyone has their own agenda. It isn't black and white."

"Why did you teach me how to use my magic?" I demanded. "*Why?*"

"Trust," she replied, her features twisting. "I'm sorry, Skye, I had to get you to let down your guard. *I had to.*"

"You had plenty of opportunities," I said, trying to buy time or find a hole in her plan I could exploit. If I didn't get out of this before she broke the curse, we were all up shit creek. "Why didn't you take me the day you found me asleep by the hawthorn?"

Lucy didn't reply, she just narrowed her eyes and began readying herself for the ritual.

No witch in their right mind would team up with Carman unless there was some kind of reward or leverage involved. *C'mon, Skye, think!*

Nightshade Witches had a grudge against the Crescents. Was it just because they wanted to rid the world of the one thing that was keeping Carman from returning and unleashing Armageddon? Or was it something more?

"She took something from you, didn't she?"

Lucy stiffened.

"That's what you were talking to the fae that had stolen Alex's face about that day," I went on. "He was threatening you."

She rolled her eyes and continued her way around the clearing, setting up for the ritual. I could sense her magic every time she stopped. She was anchoring something in the shape of a pentagram. The four earthly elements—earth, air, fire, water—and the final element, spirit, to the symbol's the fifth point.

"She has your family." I guessed. "Am I right?"

"You have to do what you have to do," she said. "And so do I. I'm sorry, Skye, I really liked you, but they're more important to me than you'll ever be."

I would like to think she didn't want to betray me—it was a comforting thought in the face of the battle to come—but Lucy felt she had to follow through with Carman's demands to save her family…but she could still change her mind. It wasn't too late.

"Your family might've done bad things, but you don't have to," I said, begging. "You can be different, Lucy."

"They're still me family!" she exclaimed. "She has me mother, me grandmother, me aunt, and me little sister! A fifteen-year-old kid!"

"Your sister is innocent, but everyone else murdered my family! They burned them alive, did you know that? Three Crescent Witches strung up and *burned alive*. And their death took my mother from me when I was a child.

After all that, I still want to help you. *Please, Lucy*. We can beat her. We can get your family back, and Carman will get what's coming to her. We won't have to hide anymore. No one will!"

"*Shut up!*" she said, screeching.

"Carman will be gone, and we can come out of hiding," I said, searching for my magic. "We could celebrate what we are, openly. We could use magic anywhere. Together, we could live in peace. If you do this, magic will die. Carman will take everything you are and use it for her own ends. Even if you save them—"

"I said, *shut up!*"

Her palm connected with my face with a crack, and I gasped.

"And don't even try to look for your magic. I've locked you out. That was the first thing I did."

"Lucy, please…"

"She took their magic," Lucy said, her fists trembling. "She was just as bad as Carman, so why would I trust you? Crescent *spawn*."

I faltered. So that was Aileen's revenge. She'd confronted the coven who'd murdered her family and hadn't delivered death but something far worse. She'd taken the Nightshade's birthright as punishment, only sparing Lucy and her sister. Mercy that hadn't been appreciated considering my current predicament.

Lucy had spent her whole life growing up with a destroyed family, and to her, Aileen had been to blame. I saw it now.

She had a chance to change but had chosen the path her family had set her on. Their bitterness and hatred had shaped her, and so here we were.

Lucy had played me all along. Here I thought all

witches were on my side, and the only tricksters in the equation were the fae. Revenge was a slippery slope.

There was no changing Lucy's mind. It had already been made up long before she met me.

"So, how's this going to go?" I asked, staring at the darkness above. "Do you slit my wrists and do your little slam poetry performance while I bleed out? Are you just going to leave me tied up here and let my body rot? That's just asking for a forensic analysis by the cops, FYI. I bet your DNA is *all* over the place. Don't forget to scrub me down with bleach by hand! Because I'm pretty sure magical scrubbing brushes are against witchy laws since I'm not allowed to have spelled knitting needles. And I really wanted one of those funky jumpers for Christmas. You know the ones with the reindeer and tinsel and bells and shit sewn on the front? Man, imagine what the pictures would've been like."

"Don't waste your last moments on pointless dribble, Skye," Lucy said. "It's not becomin' of a Crescent Witch. At least our ancestors knew how to die with dignity even when they were lashed to stakes."

"And how will you live with yourself, Lucy?" I asked, glaring at her. "Knowing you betrayed your entire kind to the greatest evil who ever lived? When you're all writhing in agony at the mercy of the fae, you'll look back to this moment and know all that suffering was because of you. *It will be your fault.*"

She laughed and shook her head. "You really don't know anythin'. It's unbelievable."

"What? What are you talking about?" I demanded, trying desperately to hold onto consciousness. "*What do you mean?*"

Lucy began to chant, her words sounding alien to my

ears. I couldn't concentrate as her magic swelled, then settled over me like a blanket. Everything was muffled, and I couldn't move. I couldn't even struggle or scream.

I was completely helpless.

Lucy stood over me, holding the dagger in her hands. Her gaze met mine, and I knew there was no getting out of this. Not like before, when I'd still held onto a sliver of hope. No, this time I knew. The clarity was startling, and I resigned myself to my fate.

I'd done all I could, hadn't I? I'd been dumped into all of this Crescent Witch business with no warning, no guidance, and no clue. Dumb luck. That was what it had been all along.

Dumb. Luck.

I cried out as Lucy dragged the dagger along my arm. From wrist to elbow, she sliced me open, opting for the overkill method. Then she gave me a matching slice.

I felt blood oozing from the wounds, and my head swam. I was so tired… My arms burned, yet I felt so cold.

"I'm sorry…" I said through a moan. "Aileen, I'm so sorry…"

Lucy continued her chanting, raising her hand and swiping her bloodstained thumb across my forehead.

"Goodbye, Skye," she murmured. "Thank you, for your sacrifice."

The world was torn away, and I fell. I was twisted inside out, back to front, and catapulted from side to side. Then I landed on my feet.

Gasping, I held out my arms to steady myself.

That was when I realized the cuts were gone. So was the pain. *Freaky*. Was I dead and in the afterlife?

Looking around, I found myself in a dark room. The walls were made of large bluestone slabs, and the only light came from some flaming torches set along the wall in wrought iron sconces. It was very medieval in there.

There were two large wooden doors set into the walls on either side of the room, complete with black iron embellishments. Totally fancy hinges and handles and shite.

Striding over to the right-hand side, I wrestled with the loop, the ancient mechanism doing my head in. Finally, I figured out I had to raise the ring and turn it to the side to unlatch it.

Opening the door, I ran through, determined to get out of there, then skidded to halt as I ran straight back into the room I'd been in. *The hell?*

Turning, I went back the way I'd come and cursed when I realized I was standing on the opposite side of the same room. Still, I tried both doors several more times, all with the same result. Predicament *confirmed*.

I didn't have to be a genius to know I wasn't in Kansas anymore.

I wished Boone was here. Boone would know what to do. He would have to know I was missing by now, and he'd be searching. And Mairead... Mairead! I was supposed to help her with her drawings tonight. *Dammit.* Talk about messing up a lovely night at home in front of the heater.

Like any of that mattered now. If this was my eternal resting place, it totally sucked balls!

"So, this is who all the fuss is about."

The silky voice oozed over my skin, and I shivered in revulsion. It felt like I'd been dipped into a vat of slime like a tea bag. *Gross.*

Turning, my gaze locked with a woman who'd appeared at the other end of the room. Where she'd come from, I didn't know, but my mind clamored with an odd sensation of déjà vu.

Giving her the once-over, I took a step back. She was as tall as me, her frame willowy and lithe. Her brilliant green eyes were framed by long lashes and cascading auburn hair. Freckles dusted over her cheeks, giving her an ethereal look, but her mouth let her down. It was hard and spiteful, twisted into a sneer that sent a bolt of dread into my heart.

She took a step forward, her emerald-green dress flowing in soft waves, and I took another step back.

"Do you know who I am, *Crescent*?"

There could only be one person who wanted to drag me down with her poisonous claws and be present for my last breath.

"You're Carman?" I asked, raising my eyebrows. "You're not much to look at."

"Arrogant, insolent…" She narrowed her eyes and regarded me with a disdain that was palpable. "I see a thousand years has not dampened your wit, Crescent."

"I'm twenty-eight," I replied, not caring if I peed her off or not. "Which is so much more youthful than a withered thousand-year-old husk. Nice glamour spell, by the way." I held up my hand and gave her the thumbs up. "Impeccable. No one likes to go down to the shops and see a walking mummy wheeling around a shopping trolley. They have museums for that these days. Hey, do you know what an iPhone is?"

"*Silence!*" Carman screeched, the force behind her voice knocking me on my ass. *Literally*.

Luckily, it didn't hurt since we were in a magical *vision-esque* plane of existence. A mirror reflecting a mirror, *etcetera, etcetera*.

"Wow," I said. "You call me arrogant? You're the one

who's standing there waiting for the moment I die. You could've been happy with just knowing Lucy had done her job, but no, you had to come and gloat."

"I did miss the barbecue," Carman said. "I hear the flames rose higher than the forest canopy."

"*Bitch*," I said with a snarl, pushing to my feet.

"I've been called worse. *Much worse*."

Her smile was sweet, and it made me want to vomit. This might be the end for me, but Boone would never let her win. *Never*.

"You may get back into Ireland after I'm gone," I said, "but you'll never open the doorways. *Never*."

Standing beside me, she caressed my face, regarding me with an icy glare. "For the last Crescent, you are quite disappointing. The culmination of your coven's power has let you down, child. I sense her in you, but she hasn't come forth."

"Who are you talking about?"

"It's a shame," Carman said, ignoring my question. "I would've liked to, how did you say it? *Gloat* to her one last time."

"Gloat to who?" I demanded. "What are you talking about?"

Carman smiled, her green eyes sparkling in triumph.

"Skye Williams, the last Crescent Witch. It has not been a pleasure." She waved her hand through the air. "May you forever lie restless, knowing you failed everyone you love."

The room began to shimmer, and I lunged toward her with a roar. "*Don't count on it, you bitch!*"

My fingernails scraped against her cheek, and then I was falling through darkness. Plummeting and tumbling… until I wasn't anymore.

CHAPTER 19

G asping for air, I raised my head.

Firelight shone around me, the air icy and full of the scent of wood smoke and damp earth.

"Does she know?" Lucy asked. "Does she know about you?"

I was back in the clearing, alive and… *Ow, my arms sting like a motherf—*

"Let her go, and we might spare you," a familiar voice boomed.

"I can't do that, Boone. It's too late."

Boone! I struggled against my restraints, searching for my magic, but it was still locked inside. I wasn't dead! There was still a chance to stop the curse from being broken. I just had to get out of here.

I kicked and wriggled, trying to ignore the burning pain in my arms. My strength was waning, my attempts at escape making me look like a fish out of water, flopping around uselessly on a riverbank. Yep, that was me. Skye Williams, *sucker*.

"This is your last warnin'," Boone said, his voice taking on the quality of an angry animal.

"And you've already had yours!" Lucy said, roaring in frustration and twisting toward Boone.

I sensed the build up of magic inside her, and my eyes widened.

"*Look out!*" I screamed.

He'd anticipated it as well but didn't react fast enough. A blast of magic struck him square in the chest, and he flew across the clearing. He collided with a tree, his head whacking against the trunk with a thud.

"I don't have time for this!" Lucy said, her fists shaking with rage. "Stay out of me way!"

She turned back toward me and raised her hands, focusing her magic on the ritual. A purple shimmer erupted around the clearing, and my gaze met Boone's. She'd invoked a barrier, locking him out.

I pulled against my restraints, desperately trying to break free. I called on my magic, but the golden ball sputtered and died, only reaching the size of a pea before it was squashed.

No! It couldn't end like this.

"*Skye!*" Boone howled in agony, his fists beating on the barrier, sending purple flares rippling through the air.

"It's okay," I said, longing for one last kiss. "Boone, it's okay…"

"No!" he bellowed, beginning to shake. "*No!*"

His entire body erupted, his change overcoming him so fast he'd turned in a blink of an eye, but when I saw the shape he'd formed, my mouth fell open.

A large, gray wolf stood outside the barrier, his chest and paws snow white, and his eyes a startling shade of amber. He was massive, at least the size of… *The wolf that had attacked me.* There were so many things wrong with what was happening, but I didn't have the strength to ponder the implications.

"Holy fu…fruitcake," I exclaimed, causing Lucy to turn.

Wolf-Boone snarled, baring his razor-sharp teeth, and lowered his head in warning.

"No… You're… You can't be!"

The wolf stepped forward, tearing through the barrier like it wasn't there at all. It flared purple, then sputtered before dying completely.

I stared in shock as he advanced on Lucy like the Terminator. Menacing, without fear, and with deadly intent.

She raised her hands, calling on her magic, and I opened my mouth to scream a warning, but Wolf-Boone had felt it, too.

His jaws snapped, and he sprang forward, his haunches launching him off the ground at an alarming speed. He collided with Lucy, and she fell onto her back with him on top. His jaws snapped and…

I turned my head away as the witch screamed, the sound of tearing flesh and crunching bones making me want to hurl.

"Stop!" I screeched, tears streaming from my eyes. *"Boone, stop!"*

My magic flared, and the restraints holding me down were broken. Lucy's magic had been severed, which meant…

"Oh, God," I whispered, rolling onto my side. I heaved, but my stomach was empty.

Dragging myself off the stone slab, I glanced up at

Boone, who'd stopped his frenzied attack and was now staring at me.

"Boone…"

His eyes fixed on me, sparkling in the torchlight. His fur was matted with blood, and his teeth were red with it.

"It's over," I went on. "You can change back now…"

Trying not to look at what was left of Lucy, I crawled toward him.

The wolf lowered his head in warning, a low growl coming from his jaws. I hesitated, my fear almost getting the best of me, but I wasn't backing down. Despite all his animal instincts wanting to take over, Boone was still in there.

Reaching out, I ignored his deepening growls and grasped the fur behind his ears. The moment I touched him, I felt my magic snake through my arm and flow into his body.

The effect was immediate. The tension seeped from him, and he whined, his head rubbing up against mine. Nestling beside me, his snout nudged my arm, and then his tongue lapped at the cut. I shivered, fearful he would lose control and chomp down on me at any moment, but he didn't. The touch of Crescent magic had called him back, and he was little more than a puppy. The wild wolf had been put back into his box…for now.

"I'm okay," I whispered to the wolf. "I need you to come back."

He blinked and lowered his nose.

"*Please.*"

He whimpered softly, then his bones began to crack as his body went through his change.

I sat back on my heels. I never liked seeing him go through it, but I'd also never seen him as a wolf before.

Back when I'd first found out he was a shapeshifter, I'd asked him why he only had a few animals in his arsenal. His answer had been surprising and kind of alarming. He never tried until was sure he could change back.

Holding my arms against my stomach, I waited as his snout shrunk and his fur disappeared. I waited until his humanity began to show before I sighed in relief.

Finally, he knelt before me, naked as the day he was born—covered in the blood of the witch who'd betrayed us—and began to shiver. I opened my arms, ignoring the sting of my own wounds, and held him against me.

"Who am I?" he whispered, clinging onto me for dear life. "What have I done?"

"What you had to," I replied.

"I killed her…" He was on the verge of hysterics.

"Boone, listen to me," I said, grasping his face in my hands. The cuts on my arms didn't seem to hurt as much anymore. "You did what you had to. Do you understand what she was trying to do?"

He nodded, his bottom lip quivering. "She was tryin' to break the curse."

"Which means she wasn't our friend. She was never here to help us."

His expression faltered, and he reached up and grasped my wrists. "Skye… Your arms…"

"Huh?"

Glancing down, I gasped as I saw the cuts Lucy had opened up with her dagger had begun to knit back together. All that remained were two long puckered lines. How… Wolf-Boone had licked them like a lollypop!

"So you have a magical tongue now?"

"I don't know how… I didn't know I could… That's not one of me shapes."

It may not be, but he had a whole past he knew nothing about. He probably had the ability to change into a whole menagerie, and he wouldn't even know.

"We can try to piece together this later," I murmured. "Right now, we need to go home and prepare."

"For what? We stopped the ritual… Didn't we?"

I frowned and lowered my head.

"Skye?"

Grasping Boone's hand, I rose to my feet. I wasn't so sure, but there was no way of knowing until it was time for the ultimate showdown. Even if we dodged a bullet this time, there would be another attempt, and another, and another until one of us got what we wanted.

Boone was looking up at me expectantly, but we had bigger wolf-sized fish to fry right now.

"Let's go home," I murmured. "Before you catch a cold."

CHAPTER 20

I didn't let Boone shift for our walk back to the cottage.

Gathering what was left of his clothes, I bundled him up and made him sit outside the clearing. While he shivered in his undies, I cast one last spell.

I wasn't sure if I should thank Lucy for the lessons she'd taught me, but it was her guidance that saw me wipe my hand across the whole scene…and erase it. The pools of blood dissolved like a pot of boiling water that had completely evaporated, steaming and bubbling until it was no more. The torches were snuffed out and began growing leaves and branches, the earth taking them back into the soil.

And Lucy… The ground took her, too.

Moss, lichens, and grass sprouted over the mound, growing and spreading until the entire scene looked as if it were part of the forest once more. Only Boone and I knew that under the uneven surface lay the witch who betrayed all of us. There her cairn lay like the ancient burial mounds that were dotted all over Ireland.

I didn't say any words, I didn't use any anchors, I didn't

even use any potions or elixirs. All I had at my disposal was my heart. Instinctual magic, she'd called it. The most unpredictable kind there was.

I waved my hand, and just like that…the horror was gone.

***

Mairead was waiting for us at the cottage when we returned.

"Oh, *cac*," she exclaimed when she saw Boone and me.

We were covered in blood. Our clothes were stained with it, but by the time we'd reached the village limits, the gashes on my arms were nothing but pale pink lines.

She began fussing as she hurried us inside, making sure the door was locked.

"I was so worried," she exclaimed. "When Boone rushed off like that…"

I glanced at him.

"When you didn't come back, I began to worry," he said. "Then I sensed magic in the forest."

"He ran right out of here like his ass was on fire," Mairead added. "What happened? Are you hurt?"

"It's a long story." I sighed, not wanting to get into it right now. Turning to Boone, I added, "You better get into the shower and warm up."

He glanced at Mairead, then back to me. Finally, he nodded and shuffled upstairs. A moment later, the bathroom door closed, and the sound of running water rushed through the old pipes.

"Skye… What happened?"

I glanced at Mairead, knowing I was babying her a little. She was eighteen and a woman now, but I still saw her as the kid sister I never had. Especially now she was living under my roof and had been attacked by the same creatures who were hunting me.

"I can handle it," she said firmly.

"I know, it's just… It was a close call tonight." I shook my head, wanting nothing more than to hash it out with Boone.

"You're covered in blood…"

"I'm okay, Mairead," I said firmly. "Boone is a little shaken up, so I want to check on him. Could you boil the kettle for us? I think I need a hot cup of tea…with some whiskey in it. At least a fifty-fifty ratio of the stuff."

Her bottom lip trembled, but I knew well enough that it was more to do with the scare we'd put her through than being offended at the lack of an explanation.

I slid my arms around her neck and hugged her tightly, though it was a full thirty seconds before she embraced me back.

"Thank you," I whispered into her ear. "I always wanted a sister, you know."

"Really?"

"Yeah."

"Me, too."

Letting her go, I shooed her into the kitchen. Kicking off my boots, I left them by the front door and padded upstairs to find Boone.

Knocking softly, I opened the door and shuffled into the bathroom. He was standing in the bathtub, water from the shower head pounding on his shoulders. The curtain was askew, and a fine mist was dampening the mat on the floor. Fixing it, I clucked my tongue as my socks soaked through.

"Why a wolf?" he murmured, not turning around.

"I don't know," I replied, perching on the end of the bath and wetting a face washer.

"Apart from the time I stopped the wolf from attackin' you, I've never seen or touched one."

"They're meant to be extinct," I said. "Mary Donnelly told me there are no more in Ireland."

"Which means the wolf was a shapeshifter."

"Yeah, well, he's a one-eyed shapeshifter now." A pang of nausea wobbled through my gut at the thought it had been a man stalking me that day in the forest. "Besides, he never came back."

"As a wolf."

"Not helping," I said, giving Boone a side-eye glare.

"The truth is… I could've been anythin' before."

"You could've been a slimy toad for all we know," I said, dabbing at the dried blood on my arms. "You said it yourself, your powers are still developing. Or at least, you're discovering what you're already supposed to know. Didn't you say once that you didn't know you could empathize with an animal's emotions until the day you saved Roy from Bully?"

"Yeah, but—"

"No buts," I scolded. "There's no use panicking until we have to, and even then, panicking isn't the best use of our time."

He turned, his eyebrow quirking.

"I'm finding it very hard to reassure you while you're standing there naked."

"I should be reassurin' you," he said. "You were the one who was almost sacrificed."

My cheeks flushed, and I looked away. The pain in my arms had been unbearable, but the gashes weren't as deep as the hole Lucy's betrayal had carved out of my soul. The witches were supposed to be with me, not against me.

"Boone…" I glanced up at him. "I saw her."

"Who?"

"Carman."

He dropped the soap, and it hit the bottom of the bath with a *plop*.

"Right before you showed up, I was drawn into a vision or whatever it was. I was in a room… There were two doors, but every time I walked through them, I was back in the same place. Over and over. Then she… She spoke to me." I grasped his hand.

"What did she say?"

I shivered despite the steam that had built up in the little bathroom.

"She thought she'd won," I murmured. "She thought…"

"Well, she was wrong."

"It's real now," I said. "I mean, it always has been, but now Carman has a face."

Boone was silent, and I didn't blame him. There was nothing he or anyone else could say to make this any better.

"Everything is so messed up," I said. "Even the hawthorn tried to warn me, but I was too stupid to listen until it was too late."

"The hawthorn?"

"Right before Lucy… I placed my hands on the tree, and it showed me a vision." I snorted and flung the face washer into the bath. "It wasn't the first time."

"What did it show you?"

"Lucy was a Nightshade Witch," I said. "Her family… The people she was trying to save by taking me… They were responsible for murdering the last of the Crescent Witches. They took Aileen's family, and that's why she was called back to Derrydun, leaving me behind with my dad."

"They were your family, too, Skye," Boone murmured.

"The hawthorn was trying to tell me something," I said.

"It was warnin' you about Lucy," he said, his brow furrowing.

"Yeah, but why did it shove me into the ground like that?"

"What are you talkin' about?"

"I was Aileen. Aileen was me. In the visions. Nineteen eighties Derrydun was weird."

Boone tensed and turned off the shower. He still didn't like it when I brought up how Aileen had died as he was carrying around misplaced guilt that he was to blame. She'd forgiven him in her last moments, and so had I once I'd learned the truth. We lived in troubled times.

"You…" he began, but I threw a clean towel, and it hit him in the face, stopping him from saying any more.

"It doesn't matter."

I held up my arms and studied the pink lines. Whatever Boone had done, it hadn't worked entirely. I was still stuck with a physical reminder of what had happened in that clearing.

"I'm going to get tattooed," I declared.

"To cover those little things?" he asked.

"Boone, I need to go back to the hawthorn," I said as he wrapped himself in the towel. "I need to make sure."

"Sure of what?" He stepped out of the bath and gestured for me to undress so I could wash off the night's escapades.

"The ancient hawthorn in the forest holds the

memories of the Crescent Witches," I said. "Or at least, I think it does. They're trying to tell me something. Something important. I think it could help with what's coming."

"Then we'll figure it out."

"I'm afraid we didn't stop the ritual in time," I went on, my words beginning to run into each other. "If that's true…"

"*Shh*," Boone murmured, grasping my shoulders. "We'll go back, but not tonight. Tonight we rest, okay?"

I nodded, knowing I was on the verge of hysterics. I'd kept it together so well… Boone was a wolf, I was the key to breaking an ancient curse, my family had been burned alive, I'd had a taste of Aileen's demise, Lucy had betrayed us all, I'd almost died, and I'd come face-to-face with Carman herself.

Talk about an eventful evening.

"Mairead's downstairs making tea," I said. "There's whiskey."

Boone smiled, but he couldn't hide the worry in his black eyes. He'd discovered more than he wanted to about himself tonight…and what he was capable of. It wasn't just about me. Not anymore.

"I'll wait for you," he whispered. "Always."

CHAPTER 21

A LITTLE MORE…

The next morning, we woke to a thick fog that had lain over Derrydun during the night.

Boone said it was just the time of year, and it wasn't an omen, but I'd been rattled to my core. Every shadow had a pair of eyes, every black cat was bad luck—not that I'd seen any cats other than Father O'Donegal's tabby—and every natural wonder of the land was a precursor of doom.

I wrapped myself in my coat, donned my beanie and scarf, and dragged Boone to the hawthorn. Mairead stayed behind at the cottage, promising to open the shop at ten.

After last night, we were all on a knife's edge.

Trees loomed out of the mist, the damp air making everything feel closer than it ought to. My toes were numb despite the extra pair of socks I'd put on, and my gaze darted to-and-fro.

Boone wrapped his arm around my waist, holding me close. His touch was comforting, as I was sure mine was for him. We both had demons to face and questions that had been answered with more questions. Hopefully, the hawthorn would be able to shed some light on the situation.

The clearing was free of the thick tendrils of fog when we arrived. Much like the tower house on the hill, this place had a bubble of protection around it that seemed to muffle all sound and give me a false sense of safety. It hadn't protected me from Lucy, after all. Maybe the bubble was to do with what had happened here.

Mary Byrne had been burned at the stake at the tower house, and now I knew three Crescents had been burned here as well. Both places had been marked by tragedy, so maybe that was what the bubble was for.

"Are you sure you want to do this today?" Boone asked, his voice sounding loud in the eerie silence.

"I have to," I replied, kissing him on the lips. "There is no perfect time to commune with a tree. Not when Ireland might be open for the taking."

He nodded and glanced up at the hawthorn.

"We have to know," I murmured, more to reassure myself than him.

"I'm here," he said. "I'll watch over you until you come back."

I nodded and turned back to the tree as Boone stepped back, giving me a little room to breathe. Placing my hands on the trunk, I closed my eyes and focused.

The last two times—and the only two times—I'd done this, the hawthorn had forced its way into my mind. This time, it was a little harder. It was silent for a long time as if it had used all its power to try to contact me in the first place. Magic took a toll, after all. Seemed logical.

Gently prodding it with my own magic, I called out. To who, I wasn't quite sure.

Light burst in my mind's eye, and I gasped. Wrenching

my hands away from the hawthorn, I turned and shielded my eyes from the sun.

My toes curled, digging into the warm sand, and I breathed deeply. The salty smell of the ocean washed over me, and the soothing hiss and crash of the waves hitting the shore lulled the transition into the vision.

Now…where had they taken me this time?

"Look!"

I glanced down to find a little girl digging in the sand with a bright yellow shovel. A red bucket had been dumped nearby, and a towel with a neon watermelon design had been half buried by her enthusiastic shoveling.

Kneeling before the sandcastle the girl had begged me to evaluate, I made a face. It wasn't very good.

"Look!" she said again.

She must've been about two or three, her cheeks were chubby, and her hand-eye coordination wasn't the best. Neither was her sentence structure.

"I am looking," I said, making a point of staring at the ramshackle sandcastle. Where were her parents?

The little girl's hair was dark as night, and her eyes were as green as the forests of Ireland. I smiled as she patted her little hands on the sandcastle. She was a total cutie in her pink bathers and blue denim hat. Neon orange zinc was wiped across both cheeks, as was the fashion. Man, the stuff stank, but she loved it when I drew little hearts and stars on her cheeks.

That was weird. How did I know that?

The little girl smiled and whacked the sandcastle with the plastic shovel. Sand sprayed everywhere, including down my cleavage, and she clapped, pleased with her handiwork.

"You little terror," I declared. "You're as bad as me when I was your age."

I stilled, my voice sounding strange. I had an accent. An Irish accent. Holding up my hands, I cursed. I had a wedding and engagement ring sitting pretty on my finger. *Man, what a big rock!*

"Swear!" the little girl declared.

"*Shh!*" I said. "I won't tell if you don't."

The girl made a face and resumed her destruction, stamping on the castle and flapping her arms.

"So, who am I meant to be?" I mused. "And who are you, huh?"

"Skye!" The girl chortled. "Mum. Skye." She jabbed her finger toward the ocean. "Daddy!"

Following her finger, I saw a tall man in a wetsuit running toward us from the water's edge. He had a surfboard under one arm, a strap connecting it to his ankle. I recognized him instantly.

"Dad?" My mouth fell open. It had been years since he'd died. Years, but there he was.

Oh, God, that was my father. He was…*young.* Glancing at the little girl, I knew it was me. Man, I'd been a smart mouthed little snot.

"How are my two favorite girls doing?" he asked, his Australian accent hitting me like a ton of bricks. He set down his surfboard and knelt beside me—I mean, the little version of me—the sand sticking to his wetsuit.

"Daddy, look!" Skye pointed to the mangled sandcastle proudly.

"Did you do that?" he asked. "You little Godzilla!"

She squealed as he caught the little girl in his arms and began tickling. I watched the exchange open-mouthed and on the verge of tears. This was our life before the

Nightshade Witches took my mother from us. We were happy…

"Are you okay, Aileen?" Dad asked with a frown.

A cold breeze tickled the back of my neck, and I shivered.

"I…" I didn't know what to say.

"I think you've had a bit too much sun," he said. "Where's your hat?"

Why was the hawthorn showing me this memory? It must be important. Otherwise…

The breeze began to whip into a full-blown gale, and I scrambled to my feet, searching for my daughter—for me. Sand was flung into the air and into my mouth and eyes. The grit stuck to my teeth, and I spat.

"Skye!"

The wind eased, and they were gone. The beach was empty, and the sky was full of storm clouds. Big, blue-black giants packed full of thunder and lightning. What a metaphor.

"I'm coming," a voice whispered.

Spinning around, I couldn't see anyone.

"*I'm coming…*"

"*Who are you!*" I screamed, the wind tearing the words from my mouth. "*What do you want?*"

"*Hold on…*"

I was severed from the vision so abruptly it took my breath away. Stumbling back from the hawthorn, I gasped, my heart racing.

"Skye?" Boone held onto me, his familiar scent comforting. "Skye, are you all right?"

I blinked, the residual effects of the vision sending my heart into overdrive.

It couldn't be. I'd felt the earth choking me as I tried to

claw my way out of the ground. The darkness was dragging me down… There was no way anyone could get out of that. Was there?

I couldn't deny it. It had been her voice, telling me to hold on. *She was coming…*

It didn't make sense, me being here if she wasn't gone. It didn't work that way!

"Skye?" Boone asked again, beginning to look rather alarmed.

"Boone…" I swallowed hard, not sure what I should feel. "I think Aileen's still alive."

Continue the Crescent Witch Chronicles in book three, **Crescent Legacy**.
Keep reading for a sneak peek!

Thank you for reading **Crescent Prophecy**!
If you enjoyed this book please consider leaving a review.

OTHER BOOKS IN THE CRESCENT WITCH CHRONICLES

series is complete!

The Crescent Witch Chronicles is a series stuffed full of Irish charm, myth, and mayhem. Come on an adventure fraught with danger and romance...and the ultimate battle to save magic before it's gone forever.

Crescent Calling #1
Crescent Prophecy #2
Crescent Legacy #3
Crescent Rogue #4

Find out more at: www.nicolertaylorwrites.com

ABOUT NICOLE

Nicole R. Taylor is an Australian Urban Fantasy author.

She lives in the western suburbs of Melbourne dreaming up nail biting stories featuring sassy witches, duplicitous vampires, hunky shapeshifters, and devious monsters.

She likes chocolate, cat memes, and video games.

When she's not writing, she likes to think of what she's writing next.

Follow Nicole Online:

Website: www.nicolertaylorwrites.com
Facebook: facebook.com/nrtaylorwrites
Newsletter: www.nicolertaylorwrites.com/newsletter
Email: nicole.this.is@gmail.com